While the waitress was leaning toward him, the man gave her a squeeze. The lady hauled back and whacked her customer, landing a loud slap on the side of his head. The man came halfway across the counter and caught the lady's left wrist, pulling her toward him.

Longarm leaped in that direction. The man drew back his hand to strike the woman, but he had already used up all the free time he was going to get. Longarm's clubbed fist crashed into his temple, and he went to the floor like a sack of flour. He hit facedown and bounced once, already out like a candle in a gust of hard wind...

→← TABOR EVANS ←→

LONGARM

AND THE INNOCENT MAN

JOVE BOOKS, NEW YORK

THE BERKLEY PUBLISHING GROUP
Published by the Penguin Group
Penguin Group (USA) Inc.
375 Hudson Street, New York, New York 10014, USA
Penguin Group (Canada), 90 Eglinton Avenue East, Suite 700, Toronto, Ontario M4P 2Y3, Canada
(a division of Pearson Penguin Canada Inc.)
Penguin Books Ltd., 80 Strand, London WC2R 0RL, England
Penguin Group Ireland, 25 St. Stephen's Green, Dublin 2, Ireland (a division of Penguin Books Ltd.)
Penguin Group (Australia), 250 Camberwell Road, Camberwell, Victoria 3124, Australia
(a division of Pearson Australia Group Pty. Ltd.)
Penguin Books India Pvt. Ltd., 11 Community Centre, Panchsheel Park, New Delhi—110 017, India
Penguin Group (NZ), 67 Apollo Drive, Rosedale, North Shore 0632, New Zealand
(a division of Pearson New Zealand Ltd.)
Penguin Books (South Africa) (Pty.) Ltd., 24 Sturdee Avenue, Rosebank, Johannesburg 2196,
South Africa

Penguin Books Ltd., Registered Offices: 80 Strand, London WC2R 0RL, England

This is a work of fiction. Names, characters, places, and incidents either are the product of the author's imagination or are used fictitiously, and any resemblance to actual persons, living or dead, business establishments, events, or locales is entirely coincidental.

LONGARM AND THE INNOCENT MAN

A Jove Book / published by arrangement with the author

PRINTING HISTORY
Jove edition / March 2010

Copyright © 2009 by Penguin Group (USA) Inc.
Cover illustration by Miro Sinovcic.

ISBN: 978-0-515-14766-7

JOVE®
Jove Books are published by The Berkley Publishing Group,
a division of Penguin Group (USA) Inc.,
375 Hudson Street, New York, New York 10014.
JOVE® is a registered trademark of Penguin Group (USA) Inc.
The "J" design is a trademark of Penguin Group (USA) Inc.

PRINTED IN THE UNITED STATES OF AMERICA

10 9 8 7 6 5 4 3 2 1

Chapter 1

"You have mail."

"Who, me?"

"What, are you an owl now? *Who-who-whoooo!* Yes, dammit, you."

"But I don't get my mail here. Not never. You know that, Henry."

"Look, Longarm, it's your mail. You do with it whatever you want. You don't want to open it, fine. Throw it away. I have a wastebasket right here you can use. But I'm telling you, it's your mail." The man seated at the desk was slightly built and bookish in appearance with his eyeglasses and sleeve garters. He was also a very salty fellow when the occasion arose. Henry was chief clerk for United States Marshal William Vail in the attorney general's Denver, Colorado, district. And he tended to go along with their jokes but in truth take no crap from the deputies who worked for Vail.

Longarm, the gent standing in front of Henry's desk, was one of those men.

Custis Long was in his late thirties. He stood well over six feet tall and had a flat-bellied, broad-shouldered, powerful build. His hair was seal brown and his eyes a golden brown. He customarily wore a tidily groomed handlebar mustache. His normal town garb, which he had on this morning, included a flat-crowned brown Stetson hat, tweed coat, and brown trousers. His boots were black, calf-high and worn outside his britches. His gunbelt was black as well. It carried a .45-caliber, double-action Colt revolver positioned just to the left of his belt buckle and canted at an angle so that he could reach it with either hand, and so it would be in the same position whether he was standing erect, on horseback, or seated at a gaming table. He was Marshal Billy Vail's top deputy, and it was no brag to say that he knew it.

But at the moment he was a mite confused. "Are you sure that letter's for me, Henry?"

"Oh, I dunno. Maybe it's for Slim the melon picker. All I know is that it's got your name on it."

Longarm shrugged. "Hand it over then. But if this is some kinda joke . . ."

"Probably somebody trying to sell you a burial plot."

"If they are, it better be in a fancy place 'cause when I go there's gonna be weepin' and wailin' and women by the hundreds show up to mourn me."

"You may be a cad and a ne'er-do-well, Custis, but you're modest. I have to give you that much." Henry opened one desk drawer after another and pawed through the contents before finally snapping his fingers with a grunt of recognition. He pulled out the center drawer, picked an envelope out of it, and handed it across the desk.

Longarm took the envelope and carried it across the room. He draped his Stetson on the hat rack that stood beside the door leading into Marshal Vail's private office, selected the least rickety looking of the chairs ranked along the wall, and helped himself to a seat. He leaned back and crossed his long legs, took a cheroot out of his inside coat pocket, nipped the twist off the end of it with his teeth, then spat the bit of tobacco into his palm. He dropped his hand to his side and unobtrusively let the severed twist drop onto the floor.

"I saw that," Henry said.

"Saw what?" Longarm challenged.

"Don't worry yourself. I'll send the bill for the cleaning crew to you. Come to think of it, maybe that's what you have in that envelope there."

Longarm reached into his coat pocket and came out with an oversized kitchen match, which he snapped aflame with his thumbnail and took his time about using to light the slim, dark, foul-smelling cheroot.

"Jeez, Custis, what did you do, soak those things in horse piss?"

"No," Longarm said, puffing contentedly with the cheroot between his teeth, "why wait for the horse piss to dry? I cut out the middle man in the deal, Henry, and just had these ones rolled up out of road apples instead."

"From the smell of them, Longarm, I can believe that."

"Either that," Longarm said, "or they were outta my usual brand and the clerk sold me these instead."

"If it wasn't against the law, I'd say you should go back there and shoot the son of a bitch that got you to buy them."

"I'd consider it," Longarm said, "but she was awful good-looking. Said she'd go to dinner with me, too, so what choice did I have? Now, hush up, Henry, and let me read my mail in peace, will you?"

Longarm tore the envelope open with his thumb, extracted the single sheet of paper inside, and unfolded it.

A minute later he stood and said, "We got nothing going on right now, do we?"

"It's quiet as that grave some cuckolded husband is going to plant you in," Henry said. "We haven't had anything to do lately but serve papers and swat flies. Why do you ask?"

"Because I think . . . I think I got something I want to do. I got some time coming to me, I think, and if I don't, well, I'll make up whatever I have to later on."

"What's wrong, Longarm? Where will you be?"

Longarm did not answer. He crossed the room, plucked his hat off the rack, and headed for the door.

"What am I supposed to tell the boss when he asks where you've got to this time?"

"Tell him I . . . Tell him I had to take off a few days. Personal stuff."

"Are you all right, Longarm? You don't look so good." But by then Henry was speaking to an empty doorway as the door leading out into the hallway swung slowly shut.

Chapter 2

The nature of his job being what it was, Longarm's battered old carpetbag was always packed and ready to go. He went back to his rooming house and shoved a handful of the rather vile cheroots in on top of his clothes, grabbed a box of spare cartridges for his .45 and put that in, then stood and pondered for a moment.

The decision made, he grunted softly and picked up the carpetbag, but left his saddle and Winchester where they were. He did not think he would be needing to ride anywhere this time out. Public transportation would do instead. And it was easier, much easier, for him to travel unencumbered by the saddle and the carbine.

There was no need for him to tell his landlady where he was going or even that he was leaving the house. She had long since become accustomed to Longarm's unannounced absences. As long as he paid his bill, which he invariably did as soon as he got back should it have come due, she was satisfied.

Longarm stepped out onto the front porch and stopped there long enough to light another cheroot—maybe he could find his favorites when he got to Cañon City—

flicked the spent match into the scraggly, struggling twigs that passed for shrubbery in front of the house, and descended the stone steps to the gravel path that led to the sidewalk.

A wave of his free arm brought a dark maroon hansom to him at a trot. "Need a cab, mister?"

"I could use one." Longarm pulled the door open and tossed his bag in, then hopped onto the steel step. He peered up at the driver on the seat above him and said, "D and RG station, please."

"In a hurry?"

"Nothing special. I have no idea when my train will be leaving. Could already have left. Not that that would make a difference. I need to go there anyhow. South station."

The driver nodded. "Seventy-five cents. Mind if I pick up other passengers?"

"Seventy-five cents is full fare, right?"

"Yes, sir."

"Straight to the station then and no looking to make extra off other riders."

"Yes, sir," the driver responded. He did not sound particularly happy about the instruction, but it was within both custom and rule, so he really had no cause for complaint.

The coach lurched into motion practically before Longarm could get settled inside—the driver displaying a bit of pique, Longarm thought—and headed across Cherry Creek toward the Denver and Rio Grande Railroad southbound terminal. The drive was not terribly long. But it was certainly farther than Longarm wanted to walk.

When the cab pulled in behind a line of others waiting there at the station, Longarm climbed down and fetched his carpetbag out. He fished into his pockets for a silver dollar and handed it up to the driver. "Keep the change," he said.

The driver gave him a puzzled look. "But I thought . . . That is, I didn't think . . . uh . . . Thank you."

Longarm smiled up at the man. "You did your job. You're entitled to some consideration. And you're welcome." He turned away and headed inside the terminal to see about a ticket.

As a federal deputy he was entitled to ride free, but at this point Custis Long did not honestly know if he was traveling as a deputy or as a private citizen. He would not know that for some time, and he wanted to do the right thing. If this turned into something official, he could always add the train fare, hotels, and whatnot to his expense sheet for reimbursement. In the meantime, until he knew for sure, he probably should pay cash out of pocket.

He got in line at one of the ticket agents' windows and passed the time waiting there by admiring a young woman in line in front of him. She was facing away from him, but her hair and clothing and figure said much about her. On the strength of her hairstyle—blond ringlets peeping out from beneath a blue felt bonnet—Longarm decided the lady would be somewhere in her mid-twenties. And she was pretty. Very pretty, in a cute, little girl way. Her figure was trim, though her dark blue travel dress was of only passable quality, which told him she was not a wealthy girl. Probably still living at home with her parents, he decided. Perhaps going now to visit a girlhood chum in . . . oh, Pueblo, at a guess.

Then the lady turned to look up toward the big regulator clock on the wall, and Longarm got a good look at her.

So much for guesswork. She was probably in her fifties, not her twenties, and her late fifties at that. She had a nose like a goose's beak, both in size and shape, well almost that large anyway. And if all those wrinkles had been ironed out flat, there would have been enough skin there to cover a saddle tree.

The lady caught Longarm staring at her. She began to blush like a young girl attracting a gentleman's interest for the very first time in her life. Quickly she turned her head away. Then coyly peeked back at him.

Oh, Lordy. Longarm found himself fervently hoping that he and this lady did *not* find themselves in the same car. Hell, what was he thinking? In the same *train*.

She looked at him again, and a hint of a smile, perhaps of welcome, tugged at the corners of her lips.

Thin lips, Longarm noticed. Lips surrounded by wrinkles.

He looked away, pretending not to have seen.

It was a huge relief, long, agonizing minutes later, when the woman reached the agent's window, bought her ticket to a destination Longarm did not overhear, and then walked awkwardly toward the waiting room benches. The lady had a pronounced limp, Longarm noticed, and carried her Gladstone bag with some difficulty.

He very gratefully turned away from watching her slow progress to the benches and nodded to the spare young man who was selling tickets for the D&RG.

"Where to, mister?"

"Cañon City."

"You have a layover in Pueblo, then you transfer to the westbound there," the agent told him as he selected the appropriate ticket forms. "First class, I assume."

"What's the difference? In the fare, I mean," Longarm asked.

"Twelve dollars," the agent said.

"Twelve dollars more to travel in first? Not twelve dollars for the fare but twelve dollars more than the standard rate? Is that what you're saying?"

"Yes, sir, it is."

"Shee-it!" Longarm groaned. At this rate his cash would be gone in nothing flat. He had not had any idea how good he had it when he was traveling on the strength of his badge alone.

Still, he had set out to do this his way and on his own dime. He would see it through at least until he knew for sure if this was official business or not.

"Do you want to go first class or not, mister?"

"Not," Longarm said passionately. "*Not*." How the hell did people afford to travel if they had to pay so damn much? he wondered.

The clerk returned the first class tickets to a rack, plucked second class forms from a different rack, and began the process of stamping and shuffling and initialing and finally collecting. He made change from the twenty-dollar gold piece Longarm gave him—not much change but at least there was some—and pushed it and the tickets through the window. "Your train leaves in, um," he turned his head to look at the clock, "in fifty-two minutes. Track one." The young man craned his neck to see behind Longarm and barked, "Next!"

The fellow next in line elbowed Longarm aside and took his place at the window.

"Son of a bitch," Longarm mumbled as he picked up his carpetbag and headed for the waiting room benches.

Chapter 3

The lady who oh so mistakenly thought Longarm lusted for her was named Lorna Emerson Leal. As she informed him within seconds after sliding onto the seat next to him. Mrs. Leal was a widow lady, widowed after thirty-three years of loving marriage.

Longarm's first thought was that her husband would be happier now. Had to be. Thirty-three years of waking up to Lorna would be enough to make any man welcome whatever it was that took her dear departed Edgar.

"Are you traveling to Pueblo, Custis?"

"No, ma'am, I'm changing there an' going on to Cañon City."

"But that is wonderful, Custis. I'm going to Cañon City also. That is where I live, you see. My dear Edgar and I . . ." The lady droned on.

Longarm paid no real attention to what she was saying. She had a low, monotonous voice that made him drowsy. Sleep would have been a most welcome refuge, but it would have been deucedly rude, so he struggled to keep his eyes open and to maintain an expression that approximated interest in the things Mrs. Leal was saying.

"Are you listening to me, Custis?"

The sharpened tone of Mrs. Leal's voice brought Long-arm's thoughts back from a *very* nice memory having to do with a chorus girl, a horse race, and a wager that paid dividends that had nothing to do with money. "Yes, of course."

"I was saying that I think a boardinghouse would be a fine occupation for a widow lady. What do you think?"

"Yes, that sounds sensible," he agreed.

"Good. That settles that. As soon as I get home, I shall start preparing rooms to take in boarders. And I am quite a good cook, if I do say so myself. Why, you should just taste my meat loaf." She launched into an explanation of the exact ingredients that she put into her version of meat loaf.

Longarm let his attention wander again. There had been that redhead who used champagne bottles, empty or full it didn't matter, to . . .

"Custis!"

"Hmm?"

"Don't you agree. Custis?"

"With what?"

"Why, with what I've been talking about for the past ten minutes. I asked if you don't agree with me about that?"

"Oh. Yes. Of course, I do." He had no idea what the hell this woman had been nattering about, but he would agree to it, to anything, if it would help to shut her up.

She smiled, exposing stained teeth and causing even more wrinkles to encircle her mouth. "Then that settles it. You shall be my first?"

"Huh?"

"My first. You shall be my first boarder. Just to help me

learn what I need to do to manage my home as a boardinghouse. It wouldn't be fair to charge you when you are there to help me learn the business, so you can stay in my home, as my first official boarder, free of charge." There was that smile again, except now it was beginning to look rather wicked to Longarm. "Oh, Custis. This is so exciting. I simply cannot *tell* you what a help you are. Why, you are an inspiration, Custis. An inspiration."

"I, uh . . ." Words failed him.

And when they stepped off the train at the Cañon City station, Mrs. Leal was clinging to his arm. He suspected she was afraid he would escape if she let go.

She was right. He would have.

"This way, dear Custis. No, not that cab. He overcharges everyone. I have a cousin who is picking us up." She turned. "Porter. See to Mr. Long's bag as well as mine, please." To Longarm she said, "It's all right. You can let him take your carpetbag. He has plenty more room on that hand truck with only my little Gladstone on it. Just set yours right on top. Right on top of mine. That's right, Custis. Just like that."

Longarm was not entirely sure how this had come about. But now . . . the woman had it all under control. Everything. Including him.

Lordy!

Chapter 4

The cousin was a heavyset, laughing soul with apple red cheeks and a brightly polished yellow hack. "Pleased to meetcha," he said enthusiastically to Longarm, without bothering to wait for an introduction. "I'm Jimmy. Now, let's put your things in the boot there and I'll have you safe at Lorna's in no time."

He grabbed Longarm's bag along with Mrs. Leal's, helped both passengers into the cab, and in spite of his bulk went up onto the high driving box as quick as a monkey going up a tree.

The hack lurched into motion with a shake of the lines and a muttered "gi-yup" from Jimmy.

When he reached the main road through town, Jimmy turned west, past the school, through the business district, and almost to the western edge of Cañon City. From his window inside the cab Longarm could see the imposing gray stone bulk of Old Max, originally built as the territorial prison, before Colorado achieved statehood. With its high walls and gun towers, it looked as much like a medieval fortress as a prison. For a moment Longarm thought they were going to pass it, but Jimmy turned left,

away from the highway, and rumbled across one of the
two bridges that crossed the swift-flowing Arkansas River
at Cañon City.

Past visits had taught Longarm that while both bridges
ultimately connected with the road leading back toward
the town of Florence and the Old Soldiers Home, com-
moners like himself were more likely to use the lower
bridge than this one. The homes at this end of town tended
to be large and fancy and belong to the better classes. He
had seen them only from a distance and that usually from
the other side of the river.

"We're almost there," Lorna assured him when Longarm craned his neck and tried to look back toward the
prison side of the Arkansas.

A moment later she squealed with delight as Jimmy
guided his hack onto the graveled driveway of a stately,
two-story house that had porches top and bottom and a
pair of huge larch trees flanking the walk. "We're here,
Custis. Come along now. Jimmy, you can set the bags
inside. That's a dear. Thank you."

By then she had Longarm by the elbow and was practically dragging him along with her, up the steps onto the
porch with its wicker furniture, through the vestibule and
into a dark, ornate entry with a staircase immediately in
front, a parlor to the right, and a wood-paneled study lined
with bookcases to the left. An upright piano sat against
the wall immediately below the stairwell banister, while a
hallway ran back from the foot of the stairs. If things ran
true to form, Longarm guessed, the kitchen would be back
that way, as would a dining area and possibly stairs going
down to a basement if one had been dug. Upstairs would
be the bedrooms, the number of those depending on their
size and positioning.

It was a fine house. Handsome. And obviously expensive. Whatever the lately departed Mr. Leal had done, he had done it damned well. Or so one would assume from the house he'd built.

"Do you like it?" Lorna asked almost immediately.

"Oh, yes. It's mighty nice. Mighty nice indeed."

"You can take our things upstairs. Just drop my bag in my bedroom, if you please. And pick out whichever room you want for yourself. I'll get started with a bite of something for dinner. You must be hungry after your trip."

"That, uh . . . Sure. That'd be fine."

Lorna flashed a smile at him, dropped her bonnet onto the piano stool, and disappeared in a flurry of rustling skirts toward the back of the house.

Longarm turned around. Jimmy was still standing there beside the bags, shifting awkwardly from one foot to the other.

"Is there something else?" Longarm asked.

"Yes, dammit. The old cow said she'd pay me to pick her up. Did you see so much as a penny change hands here?"

Longarm sighed. And paid the man. Lorna's cousin, huh?

Jimmy let himself out. Longarm picked up his bag and Lorna's and trudged up the stairs with them. In the second-floor hallway, its short length lined with portaits of people Longarm did not recognize, he set his carpetbag down and carried her Gladstone to the open doorway on his left. That room was barren except for some basic furniture, so he tried across the hall and found what was quite obviously the master bedroom. It held a massive four-poster, a dressing table covered with jars and bottles—scents, he assumed, and cosmetics—and an over-

sized wardrobe that would have been a bitch to get up
here on the second floor. They might have had to winch it
up to the balcony somehow and bring it in through the
glazed double doors on that side of the room. He depos-
ited Lorna's bag on the floor there and stepped back into
the hall.

There was one other bedroom behind a closed door,
that one also furnished but with no bedding on the bare
mattress. Another door hid a water closet that was
plumbed to evacuate water, presumably discharging into
the nearby Arkansas, although water had to be carried up
in buckets in order to fill the overhead tank or for washing. And a final door covered only a linen closet that had
sheets and towels neatly stacked out of sight.

On a whim of curiosity Longarm went back to the water closet, stepped up onto a stool provided for that pur-
pose, and dipped a hand into the water tank. It was full.
So probably Lorna had a servant girl who took care of
mundane household tasks like that.

If the lady could afford this house, complete with one
or more servants, it seemed odd that she would be thinking of turning it into a boardinghouse. And if she did, she
could not hope to bring in very much income with only
the two bedrooms available to let.

Not that it was any of his business, Longarm reminded
himself.

He set his bag inside the bedroom closer to the stairwell and went back downstairs. He intended to wander
back to the kitchen to keep Lorna company but met her
coming down the hallway toward him.

"I heard you coming down. Those old stairs creak, you
know. Are you hungry? Supper will be on the table in just
a minute. You can wash in here." She opened a doorway

beneath the stairs and stepped back so Longarm could see.

A lamp was burning, the wick trimmed low. A small water tank was mounted on the wall, with a spigot at the bottom over a copper basin. A rubber stopper allowed the water to be trapped in the basin, or that plug could be removed and the water drained out through a pipe that disappeared into the floor. A dish of soft, lightly scented soap sat beside the basin. A pair of small towels hung from copper hooks set on either side of the tank.

Longarm put the rubber stopper in place and ran some water into the basin, washed his hands, rinsed them, and pulled the plug. The water quickly swirled and gurgled away out of sight. Handy.

When he stepped back out into the hall, Lorna was still there. "This way," she said, taking him by the arm and leading him through the very ornately furnished parlor and toward a dining room to the rear.

The dining room was furnished with very heavy, obviously very expensive table, chairs, sideboard, and china cabinet. The table was set—for two—while lamps had been lighted and a candelabra was ablaze in the center of the table.

"You didn't just put this together in the last couple minutes," Longarm said.

"Now, don't ruin my fun, Custis. I'm enjoying this."

"Okay. I'll hush my mouth," Longarm said.

"Sit there, please, at the head of the table. And I shall sit opposite you at the foot."

"You gonna issue megaphones so we can talk over dinner?" he asked.

Lorna laughed and said, "I'm sure we can manage and still arrange everything properly."

"All right, then let me help you to your seat, Mrs.

Leal." He pulled out Lorna's chair, seated her, and helped her closer to the table. She waited until he had walked around to the head of the table and taken his seat before she picked up a small crystal bell and rang it.

The door to the kitchen pushed open and a girl came into the dining room.

She was . . . breathtaking. Longarm had seen some good-looking females in the past. This one outshone them all.

Oh, it could have been that he thought so largely because this one was here now and all the others were only in memory. But there was no question that this was an incredible beauty.

She was dark, her skin flawless and silky but dusky, suggesting Mexican heritage or Indian or even Oriental of some persuasion. She had gleaming black hair that was brushed back from a heart-shaped face and fell to her waist in shining waves that swayed when she moved. Her eyes were large and black and as shiny as rare jewels, her eyelashes long and curved. Her lips were full, her nose small, her cheekbones high but not overly prominent. She was slender and fairly tall, perhaps five foot nine or ten, he judged. He suspected he could put his hands around her waist and be able to touch his fingertips together when he did so.

He would not have minded an opportunity to try that.

"You may serve us now, Kiko, and when you are done with that, I want you to go upstairs and make up Mr. Long's room. He will be staying with us for a while."

"Yes, ma'am." Kiko bobbed her head and dropped into a vague suggestion of a curtsy.

"Put the good linens on his bed, Kiko. When you are finished upstairs, you can serve the coffee and see if we need anything else."

"Yes'm."

Kiko. Interesting name, Longarm thought. Could come from anything. Or just be some kind of nickname. He might ask her later.

He wondered if as well as making up his bed, she might be willing to show him how to use it.

The meal, he thought, was becoming more and more interesting. And that was without even seeing the first morsel of food on this big table.

Chapter 5

Longarm stood. Stretched. Yawned. He had spent the past extremely boring hour in Lorna Leal's parlor reluctantly playing Parcheesi. He had no damned interest in the game and spent much of the time trying to figure out just how the hell he'd gotten himself roped into this deal. He would have been a damn sight happier in some run-down dump of a hotel where he could have a card game, a bottle, and a woman . . . not necessarily in that order.

He figured playing the dumb game was a way to pay Mrs. Leal for her hospitality. But cash would have been an easier and more pleasant currency than the damn Parcheesi.

"Go ahead, Custis. It's your turn."

"Thanks, but I'm awful tired." He wasn't, but any excuse would have been welcome by now. "If you don't mind, I'll just go on up to bed."

"Very well then. You know where everything is, I hope. If you need anything that you don't see, there is a bellpull at the end of the hall. The bell is in the pantry. That is where Kiko sleeps. Give the cord a tug or two and she will come attend to you."

Now, wasn't *that* an interesting thought. Just exactly how would Kiko "attend" to him? Longarm wondered. He could think of a few ways that would be mighty nice indeed.

Might not be an entirely bad idea to wait until Lorna fell asleep and then give that cord a pull.

"I'll leave a lamp burning in the hallway so you can find your way if you need to get up during the night."

"That's mighty nice of you," Longarm said.

"Good night, Custis."

"G'night, Mrs. Leal." He went out into the foyer and took a candle and holder off the top of the piano, lit the candle from one of the wall lamps, and used it to illuminate his way up the stairs.

There was no lamp burning in the dark hall, so he went ahead and lit one himself. By its illumination he could see the gold tasseled pull cord at the far end of the hall, the cord that would summon Kiko upstairs.

Later, Longarm reminded himself. Not now. Mrs. Leal was very likely to want Kiko's services herself when she went in to bed. He would have to wait at least that long, and longer would be sensible.

The dark-haired girl with the golden skin and body as slender as a whip aroused him. He became hard just thinking about the soft, cool touch of her hair so very lightly brushing the back of his neck in the dining room earlier when she bent down to refill his wineglass. He'd gotten a hard-on then too. It was a good thing he'd had a napkin in his lap to cover the bulge in his britches.

Longarm let himself into the bedroom at the far end of the hallway from Mrs. Leal's—sensible choice, he figured, to make sure his friendly hostess did not hear any bedsprings bouncing and come to see what might be wrong—and set the burning candle down on the nightstand.

The bed had been made up with crisp sheets that smelled of sunshine, and two plump pillows lay at the head. The top sheet had been turned back ready for him to crawl underneath it. Nice, he thought. Even a good hotel would not have gone that far for a guest.

He quickly stripped down to his balbriggans, hesitated, and then stepped out of those too. He intended to be ready when Kiko got there.

Hell, he was already ready for Kiko to arrive. He had a hard-on like polished marble, veins and all. Except this marble was hot and the veins were pulsing.

Longarm slid under the sheet Kiko had prepared for him. All he needed to do now was to wait for Mrs. Leal to come up to bed—surely he would be able to hear her on the staircase when she did—then give her a little time to get to sleep. After that he could give the bellpull a yank and wait for Kiko.

In the meantime he could rest while he waited for her. It had been a tiring day, and he wanted to be ready to give the pretty girl the ride of her life.

He breathed a puff of air to blow out the candle, propped himself up on the pillows, put his hands behind his head, and laced his fingers together.

Longarm closed his eyes. And waited.

Chapter 6

The first intimation of Kiko's arrival was the very faint creak of floorboards out in the hallway. Longarm raised himself up into a sitting position. A moment later the slender line of yellow light showing beneath the door disappeared as the hall lamp was extinguished.

He heard the soft pad of footsteps beyond his bedroom door, then the very faint metallic grate as the knob was turned and the latch withdrawn. The air inside the room became infused with a flowery scent, and Longarm smiled. He gathered that the pretty girl had been dipping into her mistress's perfume.

"Over here," Longarm said softly. "I've been waiting for you."

He heard the door gently close. And the lock set. That brought another smile to his lips. Good idea, he thought. Just in case the old lady came to check on her guest in the night.

He shifted to the far side of the bed, the springs creaking just a little with his movement. He hoped that would not become a problem.

A shadow, a presence more felt than seen, materialized at the side of the bed and stood over him.

"Here," he said. "Join me."

She did. A soft, warm weight pressed down onto that side of the bed. Longarm reached out. His inquiring hand encountered flesh. Naked flesh. He heard a sigh as he drew her down to him.

She tasted of . . . berries? Something on that order of things anyway. Just to make sure, he tasted of her again, his mouth playing over her soft and very mobile lips, his tongue sliding over her teeth and into her mouth.

A hand toyed with his nipples, then slid lower, across his belly and into the thatch of coarse, curly hair at the root of his randy and ready pecker.

Gentle fingers wrapped around the base of his cock. Slid up. Down again. Played with him as if trying to jack him off. Well short of ruining the first taste of pleasure, the fingers withdrew.

The bed shifted and sagged, the springs creaking again, and the probing fingers were replaced by even softer, warmer, wetter lips.

Longarm groaned aloud as she took the head of his cock into her mouth and began to suck and lick him while her hands were busy cradling his balls. Teasing them. Promising release but giving none.

Oh, she was good. It was as if she herself could feel the taut gathering low in his groin, the sensation that presaged an explosion of cum into that wet, demanding mouth.

Building but never released, never quite spilling over the brink into that explosion.

After what seemed like half an hour she withdrew without ever taking his cum. Lifted her mouth away. Turned and settled overtop of him.

Her pussy dripped with her own juices as she reached

down to take hold of his cock and guide it inside her body as she sat down on him.

He slid so deep inside her it felt like he must surely reach her throat from the bottom up. And she was hot. Searing, or so it seemed.

Longarm moaned. And began pumping his hips, lifting to meet her downward thrusts. Again. Again. Again.

She cried out, a muffled shriek, and her body twitched and spasmcd, thc lips of her pussy clenching tight around his cock in wave after wave as she reached her climax before him.

She paused on top of him like that for only a moment then stood, turned, and once again took him into her mouth. But deeper this time. Harder.

And this time she did not stop.

Longarm's pleasure built until it could no longer be contained. He burst forth into her throat and onto the back of her tongue.

She continued to suck his juices, swallowing everything he gave her and noisily trying to draw more out.

She stopped only when the sensations became painful and he had to pull her away from his dick.

"Wow, that was . . . that was the best."

"Why, thank you, dear boy. Thank you for saying that."

The voice . . . Longarm felt a chill shoot through his gut.

The voice was not that of the servant girl Kiko. It was Lorna Leal. He was sure of it.

He felt her hand slide across his thigh in search of his cock again, but this time his erection wilted. Mrs. Leal was *not* the bed partner he had envisioned for this night.

She was, however, the bed partner he had for the evening.

He felt her mouth engulf him again and felt his prick begin once again to fill and to rise.

Longarm took one of the woman's tits in his hand—now that he thought about it, the thing was at least twice as big as Kiko's petite boobs—and squeezed. The flesh flowed beneath his fingers almost as if liquid.

As soon as he became hard again, Lorna lay on her back and drew Longarm on top of her. Into her.

Since he happened to be in the neighborhood . . . and since it felt so damned good in there . . .

Longarm began to pump and grind. This might not be exactly the night he'd had in mind, but he had to admit that it wasn't entirely bad anyway.

Chapter 7

Longarm took a triangle of cold toast out of the rack and buttered it, the butter spreading like so much yellow grease. Why fancy folk insisted on aping the damned British by turning perfectly good hot toast cold was something he just did not know. Worse, cold toast with butter and jam seemed to be Mrs. Leal's idea of a hearty breakfast.

"This evening I shall have a few friends in for drinks after dinner, dear man, so please be sure to make it home at an early hour," the woman of the house said. Wanted to show off her latest, he figured.

Kiko fetched the carafe of coffee and stood close beside him to pour. Lordy, she was a good-looking little thing. If only it had been Kiko who'd come into his room last night . . .

Longarm cleared his throat and said, "I hate to ruin your plans, but I won't be able to be here. I won't be staying. Got to get over to the prison today and then be off and moving from there, so I'll have to check out of this here hotel now, nice though it is." He grinned and winked at the old bat. "I've enjoyed my visit. I want you should know that."

Of course he would have enjoyed it a hell of a lot more with pretty little Kiko as a partner. Not that he could complain about what Lorna had given him, but a man does have his pride and Custis Long was no exception to that rule.

"Oh, but you can't go," Mrs. Leal protested. "Please stay."

"You know I'd like to, but I got my duty to perform." He drained the last of his coffee, which the pretty but useless silver carafe had allowed to cool most unpleasantly, and stood, leaving half-eaten pieces of toast on his plate. "Thank you, ma'am. I wish I could stay, but duty calls. I'll just fetch my things down an' be on my way now. Thank you again. Really." He smiled and reached for his hat . . . and breathed a sigh of deep relief as soon as he was on the stairs.

Five minutes later he was on the street and hoofing it toward the gray stone bulk of the old territorial prison that squatted on the west edge of Cañon City like some medieval fortress.

"Oh, hello, Long. Is the warden expecting you? He didn't say anything this morning about you due in."

"Hello, Charlie. No, he wasn't warned I'd be here." Longarm blinked rapidly and added, "Why. Do you boys have something to hide?" Then he laughed.

"I don't think you law dogs are supposed to see the women we keep here to amuse ourselves with, but I can't think of anything else that'd be contraband. Come on in." The old guard—he had worked at the prison practically since the day it was built, had in fact once mentioned to Longarm that he had helped to build it—unlocked the tall, heavy wrought iron gate and swung it wide so Longarm could enter.

"Thanks, Charlie. Mind if I set this in your office?"

"Help yourself, Longarm." The gatepost "office" was a stone-walled niche built into the outside prison wall, no more than six feet by four. It held a wooden armchair, a floor rack with a double-barreled shotgun in it, and something that looked suspiciously like an old nightstand with some papers piled on top and a box of shotgun shells, number 0 buck, underneath.

Longarm stepped to the open doorway into Charlie's domain, reached inside, and dropped his bag onto the flagstone flooring. He waited by the door while Charlie locked the gate behind him, then led Longarm to the courtyard end of the little alleyway that entered the prison from the road outside the imposing walls.

Charlie stopped there and called out, "Got a customer for you, Adam. Marshal to see the warden. Come escort him, if you please."

A young man wearing the dark blue coat and light blue trousers of a prison guard's uniform came hustling across the yard. Longarm did not believe he had met this one before.

"To see the warden, you say?"

"I do."

"Welcome, sir. Please come with me."

"All right." Longarm thought the boy looked like he was a teenager not yet old enough to shave, but if he'd been hired on as a guard, he had to be twenty-one anyway. It was just that the kids looked younger and younger to Longarm the older he got himself.

He already knew the way to the warden's office, but he dutifully followed the young guard—Adam, he thought Charlie called the kid—to Warden John Howard's cramped office.

"In here, sir."

"Thank you, Adam." Longarm rapped sharply on the warden's door and waited to be summoned.

"Custis! What a pleasant surprise," Howard said when Longarm stepped inside. The warden stood and extended his hand across his desk, then motioned Longarm to one of the chairs in front of it.

Longarm sat and took two cheroots from inside his coat. The act reminded him to check the stores in Cañon City while he was here. Perhaps one of them had some decent cheroots in stock. These pieces of stale shit were not worth spit, much less the cent and a half he had paid for each of them. He extended one to Howard, who accepted the smoke and provided fire for both by way of a lucifer from his desk drawer.

"Now," the warden said when both men's cheroots were streaming pale smoke, "what can I do for you today?"

"You have a prisoner here named Neal Bird, John."

The warden nodded. "That's right. Convicted murderer. Come to think of it, I believe you're the deputy who brought Bird in. That was, what, three years ago?"

"That's right. Just over that long, I believe."

"The man has been sentenced to hang. I have Bob Conrad coming in from Leavenworth to do the honors. Bob is good at what he does. He has dropped, if I remember correctly, almost a score of felons. Bob will take care of the actual hanging. I will oversee. We'll pull in some townspeople to witness. Would you like to be one of the official witnesses, Longarm?"

"I'll leave that question open, if you don't mind, John. For now I'd like your permission to visit the prisoner."

"Goodness, that is . . . unusual."

"But there is no rule against it, is there?" Longarm said.

"No, none that I know of. And we allow others access to condemned prisoners as a matter of routine. Doctors for one thing and priests or pastors of whatever denomination they ask." The warden leaned back in his swivel chair, the springs creaking a little when he did so. He tipped his head back and peered unseeing toward the ceiling for a moment. Then he sat forward again and shook his head. "Longarm, if you want to talk to the man, I don't see why you shouldn't. When would you like to do that?"

"Would today be all right, John? Like . . . right now?"

"I suppose so. Sure. Leave your revolver here, please, and step out into the hall with me. I'll ask Adam to take you to one of the private visiting rooms, then he can grab someone else by the sleeve and bring Bird to you. We need two guards to do that, you understand. It's in the rules."

"Thank you, John. I do appreciate your help with this." It really was something of an imposition, Longarm knew. The guards would have to draw shackles from the armory and take the time to fit them onto the condemned prisoner before he could be transported, even within the prison itself. Then when Longarm was finished with Bird, the process would have to be repeated in reverse. His request would take two people away from their normal duties for however long Longarm needed them. So he genuinely did appreciate Warden Howard's assistance.

"One thing, Longarm."

Longarm hoped the warden was not going to ask for a court order or some other document to support his request for an interview with the prisoner. Because he had no such authorization. "Yes, John?"

"The next time you come visiting, keep your miserable damned cigars to yourself." Howard stubbed out the reeking cheroot and dropped the smoldering butt into a trash can. He pulled a pipe from a rack of them on his desk and fetched a pouch of tobacco from a desk drawer. He was busy loading the pipe even as he walked over to the door to summon Adam back to tend to Longarm's needs.

Chapter 8

Two guards—Longarm had seen them before but did not know their names—brought the prisoner to a cold, bare interrogation room in the administration building. The walls and ceiling were made of riveted steel plate. The floor was paved with stone. The door was steel, with a small window port cut slightly below eye level. The room contained one table and three chairs, all of which were bolted to the floor.

"Stand over there, please, sir," the older of the two guards said, pointing.

Longarm stood and moved into the corner where he was directed. He waited there while one of the guards unlocked the steel bracelet from Neal Bird's left hand and relocked it around a steel U-bolt that was affixed to the side of the table that had only one chair at it.

"When you're done, sir, call out. We'll open up and you can be on your way."

"You'll be listening to what we say?" Longarm asked.

"Yes, sir, we will. Is that a problem?"

Longarm shook his head. "No, not really, but I prefer to know."

"All right, sir. We'll be right outside." The older guard, who seemed to be in charge of the detail, touched the brim of his cap and both men left. Longarm grunted and settled onto one of the steel chairs on what he supposed was normally the lawyer side of the table. The metal seat was hard, flat, and icy cold. It was not comfortable. Bird continued to stand.

It had been just a little more than three years since Longarm last saw Neal Bird. Back then, sitting behind a table with defense attorneys flanking him on both sides, Bird had seemed a wiry, alert, and very rugged young man. He had black hair cropped close above his ears and the pale forehead that comes of working outdoors but always wearing a hat, and he was sun-bronzed elsewhere on the visible parts of his body.

Now he was gaunt to the point of being haggard. His hair was shaggy and he was in need of a shave. Flecks of gray were sprinkled through his once black hair. He was, if Longarm remembered correctly, little more than thirty. If he was that old. He did not look like a well man. But then maybe the strain of waiting for your own execution date to arrive would do that to a man.

"Hello, Neal."

The young man nodded. "Marshal," he acknowledged.

"I got your letter."

Neal stepped around to the front of the chair on his side of the table and sat. "Well?"

"I don't know why you want me here," Longarm said.

"You know why, sir."

"Not really. I can probably guess. Have you talked to your lawyers about it? About an appeal, maybe?"

"They filed an appeal a couple years ago already. It was turned down."

"Then can't they . . ."

"I don't got no lawyers anymore," Bird interrupted. "Mr. Hichins left me after I run out of money. That was right after the trial. Mr. Adderly stayed with me until after the appeal, then he quit. I tried writing an appeal my own self, but I guess I didn't do so good. The court refused to accept it. Sons of bitches wouldn't even look at it. So I wrote letters. Asked the governor for a pardon. I got a printed form letter back in the mail about a month later thanking me for my interest and saying the governor was strong for justice. That sort of shit. What it come down to was that I wasn't worth him bothering with. I wrote some others too. To the judge and the prosecutor . . . Turns out he's dead, I understand. Got hisself drunked up one Saturday night and run over by a wagon."

"Yeah, I heard about that," Longarm said. "Would you like a cigar?"

"Christ, I'd kill for a cigar or a—" Bird clamped his lips tight shut and got an odd, embarrassed look on his face.

Longarm grinned. "It's all right. I know you didn't mean that the wrong way."

"Yeah, uh, thanks."

Longarm pulled one of the nasty-tasting cheroots from his inside coat pocket and handed it to Bird, then reconsidered and gave the prisoner all the rest that he had on him.

"That's mighty nice of you, Marshal. Thanks."

"No problem." Longarm dipped his hand into a different pocket and brought out the letter he had received at the office back in Denver. "You wrote this?"

"Yes, sir."

"I thought I remembered somebody at your trial saying that you couldn't read or write, Neal."

"I couldn't. Not then, I couldn't. In here I didn't have much of anything else to do, so when I was in general population, before they put me back there in isolation, I had some of the fellows to help me and I learned to read and to write passable fair."

"You can have books in here, Neal?"

"It's allowed. I don't have any myself, but some of the fellows do. They let me read what they had." Bird accepted a light for one of the cheroots Longarm had given him, then looked off toward the gray metal slabs of the ceiling. "You know, Marshal, it's a funny thing. Before I got sent here, I always thought of criminals, convicts I mean, as low, hardcase sons o' bitches." He shrugged. "And some of them are. But some of them are good ol' boys who maybe took things too far. Got pissed off and carried away with it or whatever or tried to pick up a little drinking money by selling some other man's stock. Some of these fellas are really all right. Fact is, I'm proud to count some of them as friends now. I just wish . . ." His voice died away, and when he spoke again he sounded bitter. "I wish a lot of things. Not a one of 'em means one fucking thing."

Longarm leaned forward and propped his elbows on the cold steel tabletop. "Tell me more about this," he said, tapping the flimsy paper Bird's letter had been written on.

"You heard it all at the trial," Bird said.

"I know that, but humor me. Unless you got something better to do."

"Sure. Why not?" Bird tried to reach up to scratch his nose but was brought up short by the chain that connected his shackles to the table. He switched hands and scratched the back of his neck and tugged at an ear while he pondered where to begin. Then he sat up straighter and began to speak.

Chapter 9

"First off, an' for the record, I'm not guilty," Bird said with a little twist of his lip into a half smile. "Which you have likely heard from cons before now."

Longarm responded with a snort of amusement. "Yeah. Almost always."

"Almost?" Bird asked.

"The fellows, the other deputies, I mean, we generally say there's no such thing as a guilty man in prison. Just ask any of 'em if you don't believe that's so. I got to admit, though, that I did bring in one fella, Bertram Schoenweis his name was. He was on the run for a killing. This was up in Idaho Territory. In the gold diggings. Anyway, ol' Bertram, when I caught up with him, I had to rassle him down. I managed to get the best of him and got the cuffs on him, and when I let him up onto his feet he looked me in the eye and said, 'Marshal, what I done was the same as any decent man should ought t'do. That man was in the wrong so I put a bullet in his gut, stepped up close, an' put another slug behind his left ear. If I was to do it all over again, I'd do the exact same thing, an' you can testify to that in any court o' law.' Which I did, by the way. I testified to what Bertram told me, just like he said."

"What happened to him?"

"He swung. Asshole hangman did a poor job of it though. Bertram hung there choking and kicking for ten, fifteen minutes before he finally stayed still."

"Jesus," Bird whispered.

"Uh-huh. So do you wanna tell me more about how you ain't guilty of this murder you're convicted of doing?"

"That's pretty much all I can say, Marshal." Bird ducked his head and peered down at his hands. Then he lifted his gaze again and his eyes locked with Longarm's. "All I know for certain sure is that I was paid off at the Z Slash that day. You know the outfit?"

"Just from the testimony given at your trial, but I know that much about it anyhow."

"Yeah, well, we was laying off after the fall workin' of the beeves. There was only three boys chosen to winter over, two of 'em in a line camp out toward Kansas an' just one to stay at the headquarters helping the foreman and the boss with the regular chores. Some of the boys said they was headed east to Kansas. Garden City. Over to Fort Larned. Somewheres like that.

"Anyway, we was all paid off. Maybe you know how it is. We had empty bellies an' heavy pockets, so we headed for Tipton's store, that being the nearest place where we could get a bottle an' get laid. I remember clear as clear can be the three of us—"

"Whoa," Longarm interrupted. "Remind me of what three you're talkin' about here."

"The three of us that went to Tipton's that day was me, Zenas Perch, and a old boy we all called Billy Boy. I don't know what his right name was."

"All of you from the Z Slash?" Longarm asked.

"That's right."

"This Billy Boy. I don't recall him giving testimony at your trial."

"No, sir. By the time my lawyers got to looking for him so he could testify on my behalf, he was gone. Cleared outta the country and nobody knew which way he went nor if he would ever be back."

"That's common enough in cow country," Longarm said. "Comes the winter breakup of an outfit, the boys head off every which way. They might come back the next spring or they might never. They might get themselves hired elsewhere. Get killed. Most anything might happen."

"Yes, sir. My lawyers looked for Billy Boy, but," Bird shrugged, "not knowing his proper name made it hard to find him."

"The Z Slash boss couldn't tell that about him?"

"Said all he knew was that the man came upon him at a time when he needed help. He called himself Billy Boy, and there wasn't any questions beyond that. You, uh, you probably know how that is."

"Sure," Longarm agreed. Most places, he knew, a man was whoever he said he was. The only thing anyone cared about was could he do the job he was hired for. "Go on, please. Tell me what happened."

"Right." Bird took a deep breath and finally relaxed in the chair. He had been sitting straight up throughout. "Anyway, the three of us got to Tipton's. We got ourselves a bottle. Tipton had a fat little Injun squaw in his shed out back. She smelled of lye soap more than bear grease, and she wriggled her butt good when she was humping a fellow. I've thought about her many a night since that time, Marshal. She was the last woman I had before I went behind bars."

"I can see how she would stick in a man's mind," Longarm agreed.

"There was only the one whore, so we cut cards to see who got her first. I won, so I went around to the shed and had at her. Then I come on back around to the front and . . . I think it was Zenas went second, which left Billy Boy for slippery third. We did some more drinking and I had the Injun again. I remember that pretty clear. I'm not for sure, but I think Zenas was behind me that time too." He paused to think back.

Longarm suspected Neal Bird would have relived that day time after time during the years since then. "Did Billy Boy have her again too?"

Bird shook his head. "I'm not saying he didn't. But I just don't remember, Marshal."

"That's fine. I don't want you to make stuff up. I want to know what you remember for sure. You can tell me what you think happened too, but be clear about what's memory and what you've come to believe."

"All right, sir. That day . . . like I said, we was drinking pretty heavy. Crowing some about having pussy. We got awful drunk. I guess I passed out, because the next thing I knew I was sitting on the floor there at Tipton's. My head was pounding something awful."

Longarm grunted. "Uh-huh. I been there too, Neal."

"Right. So anyway there I was. Had me a fearsome thirst on, so I went outside to the pump and ran some cold water over the back of my neck—seems that will help a headache sometimes—I ran the water and drank some of it and puked, which I already had done at least once when I was passed out."

"How d'you know that if you say you was passed out at the time?" Longarm asked.

"My shirt, Marshal. It was stinking of puke an' felt slimy. I took it off and rinsed it clean as I could get it under the pump. Then I went back inside the store. That's when I seen Mr. Tipton laying behind the counter with his head busted open and his little fat whore laying dead beside the cracker barrel. I guess I shouted. Screamed would be closer to the truth. That's what woke Zenas. He was stretched out on a pile of trade blankets. He'd puked hisself too. He got up and I showed him Tipton and that squaw. We both of us went outside so's he could wash up an' get some of the stink off himself. While Zenas was busy doing that, I went back inside to see if either of them had some life in them yet. Thought if they did maybe I could help. They was both dead. Cold as fresh-caught trout."

"What about Billy Boy?" Longarm asked.

Bird shrugged. "I never seen him again. He was gone."

"You did look for him though."

"Yes, sir. At least my lawyer said they did. There wasn't no sign of him anywhere. Far as I know there still hasn't been."

"And you, Neal? You say you're innocent, but you can't really know. You might well have done it while you were blind drunk that day. For a fact now, though, innocent or guilty, you're set to hang. How are you holding up through all this?"

"Oh, I'm all right, Marshal. You might think it's strange, but prison has been good for me. Like I already told you, I've learned to read an' write a little. The guards, they do their jobs, but they don't lord it over a man. The other prisoners mostly left me alone, even before I got put by myself in a death cell. An' the really good thing is that I've found Jesus since I was brought here." The condemned man smiled. "We got a real fine padre, Marshal. He brought me a Bible that I'm working on reading. It's hard. The words are big ones, a lot of them, but when I can't figure one out I can ask one of the guards. If they know what a word means, they'll tell me. Sometimes they'll even look a word up for me. When they go home, like. Then the next day they'll tell me what it is in plain American."

"That's good, Neal. Does that mean you'll go in peace?"

"If I got to drop, Marshal, I'll do it with an easy heart for I know I'm innocent. I don't believe I killed those people and I'm looking forward to you proving that." Bird's smile was broad. "The padre told me to pray on it. An' to send out my letters. You, you're the answer to my prayers."

"Oh, Jesus!" Longarm blurted. But not with quite the same meaning that a priest might have liked.

Chapter 10

"You're crazy if you think I'm the answer to your prayers," Longarm said before he summoned the guards to take Neal Bird back to his death row cell.

"It's all right if the answer is no," Bird responded. "As long as I know it's God's will, I can accept it. And He did send you. And you are gonna look into it and see if there's any reason to overturn the court's decision. You said you will at least look. You did say that, didn't you?" Bird's serenity seemed on the verge of cracking at that point, but the condemned man managed a smile anyway.

"I did say that," Longarm admitted.

He had spent the better part of the morning, a couple hours anyway, talking with Bird and trying to get a handle on what sort of man he was. Sincere. That was the best Longarm could come up with.

Also duly tried and convicted and sentenced to hang.

The reason Deputy U.S. Marshal Custis Long had come into the picture in the first place was because Jason Tipton had contracted with the United States Post Office to distribute mail from a rack of pigeonholes on the wall behind his store counter. That made him, in effect, a representative of the United States of America and made his murder a federal crime.

With the exception of certain military situations, there was no federal death penalty under U.S. law, but the acting assistant attorney general for the Western District, one Rufus Plumb, determined that in this case the murderer should be turned over to the state of Colorado, where he could be tried for murder and, once convicted, hanged by the neck until dead.

Neal Bird was only one of many men Longarm had over the years brought in to face death sentences. In a fair number of cases it was Longarm and his .45 Colt that meted out the punishment.

Pretty much every criminal he talked to, whether murderer or thief or confidence operator, proclaimed his own innocence. Loudly. Longarm learned long ago to ignore the claims, the pleadings, sometimes even the tears of the men he brought to justice.

But Bird . . .

How the hell was Longarm supposed to react to being called an answer to a prayer. And the fellow really *meant* it.

"Jesus," Longarm mumbled to himself again as he followed another guard out through the labyrinth of stone corridors to reach the warden's office.

"Well?" Warden Howard asked as soon as Longarm was led into his office once again. "What do you think of our jail Bird?" The warden chuckled a little at his own play on words.

Longarm shrugged. "I think he'd prefer it if he didn't hang, John. But then I'd prefer that my own self was I in his position."

"I really don't know why you bothered to come all this way down here," Howard said. "Every one of the sorry sons of bitches claims to be innocent. Do you know how many innocent men I've hanged?" He paused, obviously expecting Longarm to answer.

"No, sir. How many?"

"Every one of them," Howard said. "The truth is that I've never hanged an innocent man. Not one. And I have personally seen to the hanging of seven men. Bird will be number eight."

"If hc hangs," Longarm said.

"What? Why wouldn't he?"

"If he's right an' he really didn't kill Jason Tipton an' that Arapaho girl. What was her name again?"

"I'm sure I don't know," John Howard said. "She was just an Indian girl, after all. A two-bit whore. Really," he said. "Twenty five cents. It was in the trial transcript. I personally go over the transcripts of every capital case I get in here. That way I can be prepared."

"For what, sir?"

The warden leaned back in his chair and said, "It's a nuisance to have people in those death row cells. They are out of the way, and it takes me more manpower to guard them. Special precautions have to be taken, you know. Exercise periods have to be carefully controlled. Can't let the condemned prisoners mix in with the general population. I keep them in the regular cell blocks until their appeals have been completed. Only segregate them once that is done. I read through the transcripts so I can get a good idea whether a man has grounds to overturn a conviction or, more likely, to get his death sentence knocked down to life. Or even to time served. Why, just two years ago I had one, a Mexican he was, who got his sentence reduced to fifteen years." Howard snorted. "That one was already on death row when the word came down, so I turned him back into the population. Somebody stuck a sharpened bedspring between his ribs not six months later. He was a bad one, though, that one. I'm not surprised the other prisoners didn't like him."

"What d'you think of Bird?" Longarm asked.

"Oh, hell, Long, I wouldn't know about that. His guards would know about him, but I wouldn't. I doubt that I've laid eyes on him, not to know who he was I mean, more than three or four times the whole while he's been here."

Longarm's opinion of Warden John Howard was diminishing the longer this conversation continued. "Warden, sir, I thank you for your help. I may have to come back a time or two again if that's all right with you."

"Whatever you care to do, Long. You know I've always been a strong supporter of Marshal Vail and all you deputies. You can remind him that I said so if you like."

Longarm smiled. "I'll be sure an' do that, Warden."

Howard returned the smile and nodded, then raised his voice and bellowed, "Adam! Come take our deputy back to the front gate please."

The door to the office opened and the young guard poked his head inside. "Yes, sir."

Longarm retrieved his Colt from the top of John Howard's desk and slid it back into its leather. He had not gotten around to mentioning the derringer he customarily carried in a vest pocket or the folding knife in his pants pocket. They were certainly against the rules, but as it happened no harm had been done.

"This way, sir," Adam said, beckoning Longarm to follow.

Chapter 11

By the time Longarm got outside the cold, stone walls of Old Max, he needed two things, one a good hot meal to make up for the sorry excuse of a breakfast Lorna Leal had served, and the other a decent cigar. Well, in truth, pretty much any cigar would serve now that he had given away the last of those piss-poor cheroots he'd bought in Denver.

He left his bag with the one-legged man who ran a rooming house close to the prison. Longarm had stayed there a number of times before and knew he could trust the fellow, even though the man—Jackson was his name, although whether that was his first name, last name, or made up name Longarm was not quite sure—was a terrible one for lying. He always spun fanciful tales about how he lost the leg. Charging Little Round Top was one of Longarm's personal favorites, but Jackson also claimed to have lost it to a vengeful Sioux warrior's arrow, a Mexican rurale, and once he said it happened while he was saving a child from a grizzly bear. By chance, however, Longarm had discovered the truth. Jackson got drunk one night and passed out on a trolley track up in Denver. The streetcar rolled over his leg and pinched it off right then and there. Jackson sued the city and the trolley conductor and got enough of a settlement to allow him to open this Cañon City rooming house.

"Be here long, will you?" Jackson asked.

"Just tonight, probably."

"Then you can have number two upstairs. Those sheets aren't too awful bad used, and the man that slept in them last night looked to be a cleanly sort."

"I'll leave my bag in the foyer and take it up later if that's all right with you."

"Deputy, pretty much everything is all right with me, as you already know."

"Yes, sir, indeed I do, and I admire you for it." Longarm had once known Jackson to rent a room—on credit—to an out-of-work circus performer who brought two monkeys and a dog into the room with him. Jackson claimed the monkeys were cleaner than some human guests he'd had. But he was a little miffed because the circus fellow never had remembered to send the rent money he owed for a stay of a week and a half.

"Will you be looking for a meal now, Deputy?"

"I will."

"Then let me recommend the Widow Torvaldsen. Next block over on your left. Mention that I sent you and I'll get a discount the next time I eat there."

"And what will I get?" Longarm asked.

"A damned fine meal."

"All right. Thanks for the suggestion."

Jackson chuckled.

"Something funny about that?"

"Not at all. What I was thinking was that I already

know what you're going to think once you see the widow lady."

"And what would that be?"

"You're gonna want to see what she looks like without her dress and apron on, that's what. You are gonna take one look at her and want to tear off a piece of that. If you even hint at any such of a thing, though, she'll start in to whacking you with whatever she happens to have in her hand, so be careful what you say if she's carrying anything substantial. She like to've killed one old boy last winter. At the time he spoke to her she was carrying a poker. That was in January, and they say he didn't get his full wits back about him until April or thereabouts."

"I'll keep that in mind then." Longarm touched the brim of his Stetson and went back out onto the street.

He found a tobacconist and bought himself a supply of cheroots, remembering this time to actually light up and try one before he plunged for the bundle, then looked up the café run by the highly recommended widow woman.

The place was not especially enticing from the outside, just a narrow storefront without even a boardwalk or an overhang in front of it. The sign hanging over the door was a slab of wood with the word "EATS" burned onto it with an iron. It was the sort of place a man would walk past ten times without once seeing it.

It had, however, been recommended, so . . .

Longarm puffed away at one of his newly acquired cheroots and stepped inside the Widow Torvaldsen's café.

Chapter 12

As cafés went, this one was even more basic than most. There were not even any tables to offer comfort for the weary. Just a long counter with a row of stools—twelve of them, Longarm counted—and the stove and storage on the other side. When Longarm entered, there were three men, two of them looking prosperous and the other like a hobo who had just crawled out from under a freight car.

It was what was behind the counter, though, that held his attention. The Widow Torvaldsen was one seriously large woman. Taller than most women? Hell, she was taller than Longarm. But for all her size, her figure was proportional with her height. Wisps of blond hair escaped from beneath a plain white bonnet. He was not close enough to see what color her eyes were, but her lips were large and full and appeared quite soft, an observation he would have been willing to test by way of personal experience.

There did not appear to be an ounce of fat or flab on her, and she moved lightly on her feet, shifting from counter to stove to dry sink and back again, dishing out a bowl of something for the bum, pouring cups of coffee for the gents, stoking the stove from a bucket of coal on the floor, and then hurrying out through a back door with that bucket and another.

"I'll be right back," she called over her shoulder as she went.

Longarm helped himself to a stool at the end of the counter farthest from the front door but closest to the door leading out to the alley in back.

In no time at all the widow lady was back, carrying the coal in one hand and a full bucket of water in the other. She handled both as if they had practically no weight at all.

"What can I get you?" she asked as she passed Longarm on her way back to the stove. She set the coal bucket down beside the stove, opened the lid on the side-hung water reservoir, and poured most of the bucket of water into it to begin heating. Without pausing to take a breath, she hustled back to Longarm's end of the counter and stopped in front of him. She was not even breathing hard.

Which, he thought, was something of a pity because it would have been a pure pleasure to see those mountains under her shirt begin to heave as she gasped for breath. The Widow Torvaldsen had tits like Colorado had mountains: high, firm, and beautiful.

"I ain't had breakfast yet," he told her. "What do you have that I'd like to eat?" He made it a point to be looking straight on at her tits when he said it.

"I'll think of something," she told him, then whirled and headed back to the other end of the counter, where the two well-dressed gentlemen pushed their coffee cups aside and stood. The nearer of the two pulled a bill out of his pocket and held it forward, but just far enough from the widow's side of the counter that she had to lean toward him to take it.

While she was in that position, the gentleman, who Longarm quickly decided was no gentleman, gave the tip of the lady's left tit the sort of squeeze one uses to honk a bicycle horn.

True to what Jackson had warned Longarm about, the lady hauled back and whacked her customer, landing a slap on the side of his head that sounded like a gunshot going off. Longarm could only imagine what the blow must have sounded like from the customer's perspective. Hell, the man might lose his hearing in that ear. And if he did, it would serve him right. Longarm figured the guy was just lucky Mrs. Torvaldsen's hands were empty when he pinched her or he would have gotten it even worse. Jackson did say she hit with whatever was in hand.

The man reeled backward. His chum said something to him and the offensive SOB nodded.

That should have been the end of it, Longarm figured, but it was not. Far from it. The man who had grabbed the lady came halfway across the counter, scattering plates and silverware and empty cups when he did so. He managed to get one hand on the lady's left wrist and gave a yank, pulling her toward him and holding her there while his buddy ran around the street end of the counter and wrapped his arms tight around the protesting woman, pinning both of her arms tight to her body.

The lady's face turned red and she opened her mouth. Longarm expected her to scream but she did not. She just sulled up and tried to shake them off. The man who had her arms pinned got control of her and turned her, holding her more or less still for his partner, who leaned across the counter and punched the lady square on the tit, first the left and then the right. The blows were crisp and hard and would undoubtedly have put her on the floor had his partner not been holding her erect.

She tried to kick, but the counter was between her and her assailant. She did squeal a little, in frustration as much as fury, Longarm thought.

Longarm leaped in that direction at the same time as the hobo tried to scramble away from the counter to get clear of the tussle. The two collided and both Longarm and the hobo went crashing to the floor. Both tried to reach their feet at the same time and collided a second time. This time Longarm grabbed the hobo and threw him aside so he could resume his charge.

The gent who was most definitely no gentleman leaned toward the lady and hit her again, this time a backhanded rake of his knuckles across her face. Blood began to seep out of her nose and trickle over her lips.

The man drew back his hand for another blow, but he had already used up all the free time he was going to get. Longarm's clubbed fist crashed into his temple and he went to the floor like a sack of flour dropped in place. He hit facedown and bounced once, already out like a candle in a gust of hard wind.

"Hey, this's none of your fight, mister," the buddy growled.

Longarm gave the first man a glance to make sure he would not be rejoining the fray, then walked calmly to the end of the counter and around to the cook's side. He smiled just a little at the fellow who now shifted around so that the Widow Torvaldsen was between Longarm and himself.

"Hide behind her all you like," Longarm said. "Won't do you no good."

If it hadn't been so serious, it would have been comical, Longarm realized. The customer was a head shorter than Mrs. Torvaldsen and had to peep around from behind her shoulder in order to see Longarm.

"I got a gun," the man warned. Or perhaps he thought he was threatening Longarm with that statement. Either way it was a mistake.

"So do I," Longarm told him, pulling his tweed jacket open to display the big Colt in its cross-draw rig.

"You can't shoot me without hitting her," the man said, a touch of rising panic in his voice.

"Oh hell, I'm betting I can." He grinned and shrugged. "If I'm wrong and the lady dies, then you're the one will swing for murder seein' as how this here is a legal and proper attempt by me to arrest you."

"Arrest?"

"I'm a deputy U.S. marshal, you asshole, and you're threatening me with bodily harm. That right there is a federal offense. Plus you've broke I don't know how many state of Colorado laws already by taking that lady hostage." Longarm's voice hardened. "You on the floor. I see you moving. If you do anything other'n come easy to your knees and show me your hands, I'll blow your fuckin' head off. Begging your pardon, ma'am," he added, nodding toward Mrs. Torvaldsen.

"You," he said to the one on the floor. "Up. Now. You," he said to the buddy, "put your hands just as high as you can get 'em and come out from behind your hostage."

"Look, uh . . . are you really a deputy marshal?"

"I am."

"Look, you got to understand, we were just being playful. We meant no harm. We didn't . . . that is, we never. . . ."

"Shut up. Mrs. Torvaldsen, are you all right?"

"I will be, I suppose. Right now I hurt. In places that I can't rub here in public, if you know what I mean."

"You been assaulted and your property's been damaged. I'll let you decide. Do you want these two assholes . . . excuse me again, please . . . do you want these two *miscreants* to spend six months in jail or will you accept a monetary fine instead?"

"Six *months*! Jesus, marshal, we can't be in jail for any six months. We have jobs," the one behind the counter squawked.

"We got families," his partner put in.

"We can't—"

"Shut up, the both o' you. Mrs. Torvaldsen, what say you?"

"Are you serious?"

"Yes, ma'am. Just about as serious as a body can get."

"What sort of damages did you have in mind?"

"These boys look pretty well heeled. I'd say they can afford to pay you a hundred dollars." When he said it, he was looking closely at the one who had started the whole thing. That one did not flinch, so he quickly added, "Each."

"That would be two hundred dollars? Really?"

"Yes, ma'am. Or if you'd rather, I can see that they spend six months in county jail." He grinned. "Each."

"I . . . Yes. That."

"Which?"

"The . . . what did you call it . . . damages. They could pay damages. Yes, Marshal. Damages."

Longarm looked at the two playful businessmen. They did not look like they were having much fun right now. "Ante up, boys. A hundred apiece. Put it on the counter there." He glanced around. The hobo had long since disappeared—without paying—and would not likely be seen in this café again. "Well?" Longarm demanded.

The businessmen began digging in their pockets.

Chapter 13

"I am very much in your debt," the widow lady said after the businessmen left. She dropped her stack of twenty-dollar gold pieces into a pocket on her apron, then turned around so Longarm could not see and rubbed herself where it hurt.

"I could massage that for you," he offered.

"The hell you can," she countered. But she did relax enough to turn back around toward him, one hand still kneading the apparently bruised and painful flesh of her tits. "What can I do to repay you?" she asked. "You were quite gallant. And who knows how far they might have taken things if you hadn't been here. I really do want to do something for you."

"I'm still wanting that breakfast. Could you manage that?"

"You're awfully easy to please, sir."

"Not really." He grinned. "I just don't want to get whacked upside my head like you done to that fella, and if I say out loud what I'm thinking, well, you're almost certain to belt me one."

"Breakfast it is then. On the house."

"That's mighty nice of you." He returned to the stool where he had been sitting earlier. Mrs. Torvaldsen got busy straightening up the mess the gents had left behind, slicing ham and breaking eggs for Longarm's meal. When she bent over to stoke the stove again, her butt showed round and lovely beneath her dress. Longarm gave her ass a long look and rolled his eyes. "My, oh my," he muttered.

"Careful," she said, turning around with the poker in her hand. "You could still get a lump on your head, mister."

"Which reminds me. My mama never named me 'mister.' I'm Custis Long. Longarm to my friends."

She took a step forward and extended her hand to shake like a man. "I'm Nora Torvaldsen."

"A pleasure, Mrs. Torvaldsen."

"Nora," she corrected.

Longarm nodded. "Nora."

"I'll have your breakfast ready in a minute."

It took her a little longer than a minute, but the wait was worthwhile. The breakfast she set in front of him was hot, filling, and huge.

"Is this your regular territory, Longarm?" the lady asked over her shoulder while he was eating. She was busy at the sink washing dishes in a pan of hot water drawn from the reservoir on her stove.

"Yes, 'tis."

"Then perhaps I can count on seeing you every now and then."

Longarm grinned. "That just could be, Nora. I get down here every now and then, and . . ." He stopped in mid-sentence as something she said grabbed his attention. Territory. Deputy United States marshals do not have assigned territories. They go wherever they are directed. But some things are quite territorial.

He wadded up half a biscuit and used it to sop up the last drops of ham drippings and congealing egg yolk, then popped the biscuit into his mouth. He stood, dug into his britches, and laid two quarters on the counter.

"You don't owe me anything. That meal was on the house, remember?"

"I've decided to push for something even better than that fine meal, Nora, but right now I hope you'll excuse me. I got to go see a man. It's important."

"If you're interested," she said, "I close up about ten. Nine o'clock tonight, I think." She turned back toward her stove. "If you're interested, that is."

"Wild horses couldn't keep me away," he promised. Longarm retrieved his Stetson from the hat rack beside the front door and headed outside. He paused for a moment to get his bearings, then went off at a swift walk to the railroad depot.

The two businessmen who had harassed Nora Torvaldsen were seated on benches waiting for a train. Longarm nodded pleasantly to them as he walked past on his way to the ticket agent's booth.

"I need to get to Pueblo this afternoon and back again tonight. Can I do that?"

The ticket seller harrumphed, cocked his head to one side, and with a small smile said, "It's all right with me if you do."

"Friend, I didn't ask 'may' I. The question was 'can' I. And I'm assuming you're the fellow who's supposed to be able to tell me."

"Kidding aside," the railroad man said, "there is an eastbound passenger coming through in about twenty minutes. It will stop at Pueblo for you." Like most Cañon City locals, he pronounced the city name as Pee-eblo.

"Coming back tonight . . . let me see." The fellow pulled a
schedule book off a wall rack and thumbed through it.
"Ah. Here we go. The answer is that you can. There's a
westbound leaving Pueblo at 7:50 this evening. Will that
do what you want?"

"Yes, sir, I do believe that it will. Give me a ticket for
both of those legs, please." Longarm dug into his supply
of cash and paid the agent for his fares. He considered
going back to the waiting area and hitting up those businessmen for the price of his tickets. But then he'd already
pretty well cleaned them out for Nora's compensation. It
wouldn't be fair to make them pay again. Bastards!

Longarm walked back out to the platform and found a
seat where he could keep an eye on the two. Just in case
one of them might take exception to his methods of
achieving justice. After all, that one had said he had a gun.

He pulled a cheroot from inside his coat, nipped the
twist off with his teeth, and dipped two fingers into his
vest pocket for a lucifer. He struck the match on one of
the iron bolts holding the bench slats in place and lit his
smoke, then he leaned back and crossed his legs.

All that remained now was to wait for the eastbound
passenger coach and take that ride to Pueblo. Or Pee-eblo
if one should prefer.

Chapter 14

Once in Pueblo, Longarm found his way to a three-story red brick office building. He made his way to the second floor and entered a door with a frosted glass panel. Painted on the glass was: "The Law Offices of Winston, MacGregor, and Bayles."

A waiting area furnished for comfort with soft armchairs, gaslights, and gold-and-cream flocked wallpaper was empty except for the magazines and day-old newspapers strewn about on a pair of low occasional tables. On the far side was a glassed window area with a rather fey young man on the other side.

"Yes, sir, what may I do for you?"

"Is Hank in?" Longarm asked.

"Hank? I don't know of a Hank, sir."

"H. Ryder Bayles," Longarm said. "The H stands for Harrison, and that shortens down to Hank to them of us as knows him outside o' this fancy office. So let me ask that again, sonny. Is Hank in?"

"I, um, I shall have to go see. May I say who is calling?"

Longarm reached inside his coat and brought out his

wallet, which he flipped open to display his badge. "Tell the son of a bitch he's under arrest."

"Sir! Really, I . . ."

"Just go tell him."

The clerk sprang out of his chair and scuttled out of sight as quick as if his ass was on fire. Well, Longarm considered, maybe it was. Sort of. Seconds later he could hear a loud peal of laughter. And seconds after that Hank came out, grinning and with his hand extended.

"Longarm, you old fart. You frightened young Andrew half to death when you showed him that badge. Come on back to my office. No, wait. Forget I said that. We'll go around the corner to Clary's. His beer is always cold, and if we're lucky he'll have some oysters on the half shell. He gets them packed in ice and shipped express freight. Wonderful stuff, that."

"Damn things look like somebody hawked up a loogie and spit it onto a platter."

"They might not look so grand," Hank agreed, "but they taste just fine."

"I'll let you eat all the loogies," Longarm said. "Me, I'll drink all the beer." He grinned. "Division of labor, don't you see."

Three minutes later the two men were seated at a small table in Clary's Bar & Grill. "We'll have a pitcher . . . no, make that two pitchers," Bayles ordered, "and a couple dozen oysters if you have them. Put them on my tab."

"I can pay, you know," Longarm said.

"Not in here, you can't. Not today anyhow."

"Look, Hank, I'm trying to stay on your good side. You, uh, don't owe me any favors, do you?"

"Oh, my. It sounds like you will soon be owing me one." Bayles leaned forward eagerly. "First tell me one thing. Will this be legal, whatever it is you're wanting me to do?"

Longarm rolled his eyes and managed to look shocked. More or less. "I am hurt that you could even think such a thing, Hank."

"Of course I could think such a thing, Longarm. I mean, after all, it *is* you who is asking. So tell me."

"It isn't anything exciting. You won't be backing me up in a gunfight or nothing like that."

Bayles looked a little disappointed when he heard that.

"What I want," Longarm went on, "is for you to file an appeal. I want you to use some of that legal mumbo-jumbo like all you asshole lawyers do."

"Careful what you say, sir," Bayles snarled. "I may be an asshole, but many question whether or not I am a lawyer."

Longarm had to smile. Hank Bayles was one of the best lawyers Longarm knew. And one of the very few that he respected. "Like I said, Hank, I want you to file an appeal. Ask for a stay of execution."

"Really? This might actually be interesting."

The pitchers of beer and Bayles's platter of oysters arrived, as did a bottle of hot sauce and some pretzels. Bayles poured their first mugs of beer while Longarm continued to speak.

"Do you know Jason Tipton's store, Hank?"

"No. Should I?"

"It's way the hell out on the plains, right close to the Kansas-Colorado state line. Fella I know . . . a man I brought in, actually . . . is convicted of murdering Tipton and a Injun whore he had working for him."

"Working for . . . ?"

"Tipton. She worked at the store. Took care of the

needs of cowhands out that way. Like that. Anyway, this fella who's supposed to have killed them is over at the prison waiting for Bob Conrad to come hang him."

"I've heard of Conrad. They say he does a good job. Thorough."

"Uh-huh. I've heard the same."

"Is there a problem with this?" Bayles asked.

"The thing is, Hank, I'm beginning to think maybe Neal Bird didn't do what he's gonna hang for. I'm thinking you could buy me some time to investigate. What happened before, I was told to bring him in so I brung him in. I never had to look and see did he do the crime. Now, all this time later, I'm having second thoughts. Could be I'm wrong. Could be he really done what they say. My point is that once he's hung, there's no damn point asking did he do it. Exoneration don't do a man the least lick o' good once he's six feet under."

"What grounds am I supposed to use to ask for a stay while I appeal?" Bayles asked.

"Now I thought some about that, Hank, an' what I come up with is that Tipton's store is, like I said, way the hell out there. Likely it's in Colorado. My boy Bird was tried in Colorado. But that store, why, it could be in Kansas, don't you see. I don't know that a survey has ever been done to know for sure."

"The border was certainly surveyed," Bayles said.

"Sure it was. But the store wasn't. Not that we know of, anyhow. You could make the argument that the state didn't find out for sure if they even had jurisdiction to try the man. He maybe should have been tried in a Kansas court instead."

"That argument won't hold up."

"I know that, Hank. It don't have to. All it has to do is

to give me time to look deeper into this thing and see if maybe Neal Bird stands to swing for another man's crime. That would piss me off something fierce, Hank. Wouldn't make Bird very damn happy either."

"Give me one of those cheroots you always carry, Custis. My cigars are back in the office."

Longarm pulled out two cigars and handed one to Bayles. The lawyer struck a match and reached across to light Longarm's cheroot and then his own.

"How much time?" Bayles asked.

"As long as it takes," Longarm said.

"I might not be able to get your stay at all."

"But you might, right?"

"I could demand that the state offer proof that they had jurisdiction. There are survey records somewhere, of course, but who knows where. They might have been buried in storage somewhere since the territory of Colorado was split off from Kansas God knows how many years back. I could demand that the state produce those records. I might even demand a new survey to include that store. Tipton's, you said? Spell that for me, please."

Longarm did and spelled Neal Bird's name for him too.

"I could have some fun with this, Longarm. Hell, I might even win the appeal. I'm pretty sure I can win the stay of execution."

"How long until you know for sure?"

"When is Bird scheduled to hang?"

"Less than two weeks. They could possibly do it as soon as Conrad gets here, whenever that turns out to be."

Bayles grunted and poured himself anther beer to wash down more of the oysters. He was preoccupied with thinking about the challenge before him and this time did not think to refresh Longarm's mug. After a few moments Bayles sat back in his chair. "No guarantees," he said.

"None asked," Longarm told him. "But you'll try?"

Bayles nodded. "I'll try. With luck . . ." The lawyer shrugged and spread his hands wide, palms upward.

"I couldn't want for better'n that," Longarm said.

Hank Bayles smiled. "You owe me one, Custis."

"Aye, so I do. Now if you'll excuse me, I'm gonna finish this beer and head back to the railroad station. I got to get back to Cañon City tonight."

"You won't stay tonight? We could have a friendly game of poker if you would."

"Ha. I seen how friendly you are when you play poker, you cutthroat SOB."

"Oh, so that's how it is. Now that you have what you came for, you call me names."

"Only ones that you deserve." Longarm laughed and extended his hand to his friend. "Thanks, Hank. I 'preciate you." He winked. "But you ain't half as pretty as what's waitin' for me over in Cañon."

Longarm tugged his Stetson down and headed back to the D&RG depot.

Chapter 15

The upriver passenger train that passed through Cañon City was a few minutes early. Longarm stepped down from the soot-grimed coach and brushed himself off, then paused to light a cheroot. Lord, what an improvement these were over the garbage he had been smoking recently. He really ought to stop in tomorrow and buy some more of them.

Nora's café was still open when he got there. Four people sat at the counter, bent over pie plates and coffee. Nora looked up when the door opened. She broke into a broad smile when she saw who the customer was. "Custis. You're early."

"You know the schedule that good?"

"A lot of my customers are railroad men." She turned toward the men at the counter and said. "Aren't you, boys?"

"That we are," one of the pie-and-coffee boys piped up with. "Always happy t'get to Miz Torvaldsen's place."

"Best café anywhere along the line," another said.

"You," Nora told him, "are angling to get free coffee, aren't you?"

"Just for me." The railroader hooked a thumb toward his companions. "These mugs can pay their own way."

"Oh, get out of here, all of you."

The men laughed, and one of them pushed his cup forward for a refill.

"No," Nora said, "I meant it, boys. Out. Everybody out. I'm closing early tonight."

"Aw, you don't mean that. We ain't had our second cups yet."

"Sorry, boys. I really am closing. But you don't owe me anything for your snack. It's on the house tonight."

There was some grumbling but none of it unpleasant. Longarm could see that her patrons liked Nora and had no desire to make themselves unwelcome in the future. They gathered the lunch pails they had set on the floor, touched the brims of their caps in Nora's direction. and, however reluctantly, left the café. Longarm noticed that even though Nora had told them their pie and coffee were free, each of the men scrupulously dug into his pockets and left money on the counter, as a tip if not for the snack.

"And what about me?" Longarm asked when the railroad men were gone.

"You," she said, "can stay." She came out from behind her counter and carefully pulled down the roller blinds so the front windows were closed to view. Once that was done, she came quite naturally into Longarm's arms.

It felt strange for him to be reaching *up* to kiss a woman. But he managed it just fine. Nora tasted of cinnamon and cloves and something he was not quite sure of. Whatever it was, the combination was most pleasant. The lady's lips were soft and her tongue was active, promising pleasures yet to come.

She pulled away from him. "Let's not get too involved in that."

Longarm was disappointed. It must have shown.

"No, you fool," she laughed. "I don't mean we shouldn't get involved at *all*. I meant we shouldn't get too carried away with it right *now*. After all, lover, I have things to do before I can walk out of here tonight."

"Lover," he repeated with one eyebrow raised in question.

"That's what you came back here for, isn't it?" she shot back at him with another laugh. "You want to see if this big old gal can give a man a ride. Of course if you don't *like* to fuck. . ."

"My goodness," he said, "you're a woman as speaks her mind."

"I am," she agreed. "Now, shut up. Sit down. Over there would be good as that will keep you out from under my feet. I'll get everything tidied up and put away in just a few minutes. Most of it can wait until morning, but at the very least I have to pull the fire out of this old stove. It wouldn't do for my livelihood to burn down while I'm off draining your snake."

"I could help . . ."

"You could get a hit upside your empty head too," she snapped. "Now, do me the favor of sitting down. Right there where I told you, please. I won't be a minute with this, but it will take longer if I have to keep explaining the perfectly obvious to the likes of you."

Longarm sat. And kept quiet.

Chapter 16

Nora was as lusty as a catamount in heat. Once they were alone in the little bungalow she shared with a gray cat and a pet rabbit, she acted like she intended to swallow Longarm whole. As soon as the front door closed behind her, she locked herself onto his face with her mouth while she clawed at his clothing with both hands.

Longarm was taken a little aback. Beyond the surprise of the assault, he was more accustomed to being the aggressor in such activities. It appeared that Nora was not a girl to wait for a gentleman to take the lead in these things.

She made short work of the buttons on his shirt—such very short work of them that she pulled one completely off the fabric—and was almost as quick to get his trousers unbuttoned.

"Hold it a minute here," he said as she began tugging at the buckle on his gunbelt. "This'un I can do my own self if you don't mind."

He unstrapped the heavy belt and laid his Colt aside. While he was doing that, Nora was finishing the job of opening his britches. She pushed them down past his hips and took hold of his cock. "Damn," she mumbled. "You're hung like a fucking stallion. Why didn't you tell me, honey? I would've closed the café this morning. The hell with waiting until nightfall."

She dropped to her knees and took the head of his dick into her mouth, running her tongue around and around the head, then down the length of his already stiff shaft. "You taste fine," she said when after a minute or so she came up for air.

Nora stood then and began removing her clothing, leaving Longarm to see to kicking off his boots and getting his trousers away from his ankles.

Nora was one very large woman but her proportions were just fine, Longarm quickly confirmed. Her waist was small relative to the size of her hips and the width of her shoulders. On any other woman any one of those would have been unattractively large, but on Nora, with them all stacked one atop another, they seemed just right.

Her breasts were huge. Her nipples again were in proportion, which made the areolae about the size of demitasse saucers. The actual nipples were already hard in anticipation of the romp soon to come. They were as thick and as long as the first segment of a strong man's thumb. With that much weight pulling at them it was inevitable that Nora's tits sagged. Longarm took one look and decided he could forgive her for that.

Her pubic hair was a thick patch of dark curls that were already glistening with moisture. This was one very randy woman.

Nora saw where his gaze rested. She laughed and said, "You're wondering about the gold on top and the rat-hair brown below? Simple answer, sweetie. I bleach the hair folks can see."

"I wasn't gonna ask."

"No, but you were wondering. Now you know. Anything else you want to know, sweetie, just ask. I'm not shy."

"I was kinda getting that idea, Nora. Can I ask you one thing now?"

"Sure. Anything you like."

He grinned. "Where's the bed?"

Nora tossed her head back and barked a short, loud laugh. Then she reached for his hand. "Come along, sweetie. Let's us go find it."

"Ah. Ah. Ah. *Arhhh!*" Longarm cried out aloud as the powerful explosion of his climax swept through him. He plunged hip-deep into Nora's cunt, smashing her belly with his and clutching her shoulders until he was sure he would leave bruises. Not that either of them was apt to care about as small a thing as that.

Nora, it seemed, was one of those women who could easily reach climaxes of their own, and she had had at least four that he was sure of. Maybe more.

He shuddered as hot cum continued to flow out of his body and into hers. In the midst of Longarm's climax, Nora came again. She wrapped her legs around his hips and squeezed like she was taming a bronco. The woman was as powerful as she was large, and it was a wonder she did not break something on one or both of them.

Longarm stroked slowly in and out for a minute or so, giving the intensity of feeling time to subside. Nora shuddered again and gasped as he did so. Finally she gave his chest a push to suggest he dismount. He bent his head to hers and kissed her for a moment, then pulled out. The air was cold on his wet dick when it emerged from the heat of Nora's body. He rolled over onto his side.

"That was nice, lover," Nora said.

"Damn straight it was," he agreed.

"I don't know about you, but I could use a drink."

"Got any rye whiskey?" Longarm asked. "I'm partial to it."

"No rye, just plain old Tennessee corn."

"That'll do." He sat up on the side of the bed and stretched. All in all he was feeling pretty damn good. Relaxed. Drained. Like Nora said, it was nice. Exhausting but nice.

"How's about I cook us up some eggs to go with that whiskey," Nora suggested. She smiled. "Get your strength built so's we can go at it again."

"Tonight? Darlin', you've already got me so wore out it will likely be a week before I can convince the blind snake to let me take a piss out of it. Why, woman, my bladder could bust clean open and it'll be your fault. And won't you feel sorry once that happens."

"Nonsense," she said. "I'll bet you a five-dollar gold piece that I can get that pecker of yours standing tall again inside five minutes."

"No way," he said.

"Five minutes," she repeated. "Is it a bet or are you scared to put your money where your mouth is?"

"Huh. It's a bet," he said.

Nora chuckled. "I'm sure not afraid to put my mouth where my money is. Lay back down, lover. The five minutes starts right now."

Longarm lost the bet with three and a half minutes to spare.

Chapter 17

"You never came in last night," Jackson said, his tone of voice sounding like it was an accusation of some sort.

"No, reckon I didn't," Longarm cheerfully agreed.

"Yet you look rested," the rooming house owner added.

Longarm smiled and nodded. "Feel it too." The truth was that he had not gotten a whole hell of a lot of sleep during the previous night. And considering how active he had been through the night it made no sense at all that he would feel rested this morning. But he damn sure did.

"Find that café I told you about?" Jackson asked.

"Yessir, I did."

"Wondered what that big ol' gal looks like naked, didn't you?"

Longarm grinned. "Ayuh, I sure as hell did. Couldn't help myself. More than a mouthful, those are." And damned fine-looking when they are bare too, he could have added but did not. More than a mouthful indeed.

"You going up to your room now?"

He shook his head. "No sir, I just come for my bag." He winked. "Next time through maybe I'll actually sleep here."

Jackson chuckled and went back to whatever he had been doing. Longarm retrieved his carpetbag and headed back to the railroad depot.

"One-way to Pueblo," he told the ticket agent.

"The next eastbound leaves in forty minutes," the thin, balding agent said.

Longarm considered. He already had a good breakfast behind his belt, courtesy of Nora Torvaldsen. He had a fresh supply of cheroots in his coat pocket and more in his bag. He wished he had his Winchester with him, but it was still in his room back in Denver, and he was not going to take the time to go get it. Neal Bird had little enough time left and none to waste. No, Longarm was about as well set as he was going to get for this deal. Now he had to go about the investigation he could have done when Bird was first arrested had he only known the need for it then.

He had to determine, to his own satisfaction if not to that of anyone else, whether Bird committed the murders he was set to hang for.

Longarm sat on the D&RG platform, waiting for the next train heading east. He smoked. And he thought. He pondered the evidence that had been used against Bird and where any flaws might lie.

Longarm was in no mood to gamble about the availability of a horse. Blackwell's Station, once a stop for horse-drawn stagecoaches, was closer to the state line—and to Tipton's store—but nowadays it consisted of nothing more than a run-down store, a few houses, and a great many fading memories. He might well be able to rent or buy a horse there. On the other hand he might not.

Better to take the sure bet, he decided, and leave the train at La Junta, near the ruins of Bent's old fort.

In Pueblo he had left the Denver and Rio Grande and boarded an Atchison, Topeka and Santa Fe freight hauling Colorado-mined coal to Kansas. He had had to show his badge in order to secure passage.

"I need to get off at La Junta," he told the man— Longarm had no idea what the fellow's title or function might be, but his clothes were clean, suggesting that he was someone important—who shared the caboose with him on this leg of the trip.

"Sorry, Marshal. We don't stop there."

"You do this time," Longarm assured him. He smiled a little and began toying with a set of handcuffs he produced from a coat pocket.

"I suppose . . . just this once."

"Ayuh. Once is all I'm asking."

An hour or so later the railroad man peered out at the numbered signboards beside the tracks indicating mile markers and other information that Longarm had no knowledge of. "Five miles to La Junta," the fellow announced. He stood, picked up a red paddle, and went out onto the platform at the back of the car.

Leaning far out over the rail, he signaled the engine with the paddle and got a screech of the locomotive's steam whistle to confirm the message. The train began slowing immediately, and a few minutes later they came to a halt near La Junta, amid the crashing and clatter of couplings smashing together.

"All right, Marshal. La Junta it is."

"Thanks, neighbor." Longarm touched the brim of his Stetson, picked up his carpetbag, and climbed the short steel ladder down to the gravel beside the tracks a hundred yards or so from the La Junta depot's water tank.

The railroad man again signaled forward to the engineer, and soon the ponderous train began to roll forward once more, gathering speed until it was a dot of color quickly lost in the distance.

Longarm shifted his bag to his other hand and began looking for a livery stable where he might be able to rent a horse.

Chapter 18

He did not know exactly what he hoped to find at Tipton's store, but whatever it was . . . it wasn't there.

The front door was open, swaying a little in the strong winds that whistled across the nearly flat prairie. The inside was empty except for dust and a few empty cans. Even most of the furnishings had disappeared. Jason Tipton's big store counter was still in place, but someone had carved lewd drawings into the top. They might have been interesting except that the dumb SOB was no hand as an artist.

The merchandise, varied though it had been, was all gone now, carried off by cowhands or passing Indians or who the hell knew. Someone had managed to find a use for every lick of it. Or thought they could.

Longarm stood in the ankle-deep litter that covered the floor. He looked around, trying to see—or imagine—anything that might conceivably be helpful, but eventually he gave up and went outside.

The pump and trough were still intact, thank goodness, although the trough was dry. Likely the pump was too, and there was no jar of water left for the next visitor to prime it with.

Longarm debated with himself for several moments before he walked back to his rented sorrel. The horse's saddle was old, and he suspected the tree was beginning to crack, but the leather was oiled and well cared for, and most important, the stable hand had hung a canvas water bag on one side to balance the weight of Longarm's carpetbag.

There was still a good half gallon of tepid water in it after the ride up from La Junta. The stuff tasted like shit—like dressed canvas and sun heat actually—but it was better than nothing. On the other hand, the thought of cold water fresh out of the ground . . .

Fuck it. A man doesn't get very far if he is afraid of every little thing, and the truth was that neither he nor the horse was so dry that they were in danger of curling up and blowing away if they failed to drink again soon.

Longarm unscrewed the metal cap on the water bag and upended it over the standpipe until the last of his water gurgled its way down into the well. He just had to take it on faith that the primed pump would now draw and that the water would be good.

He gave it a moment, then began pumping the handle. After a few pulls he could feel the effort become heavier as the mechanism began to lift a column of water. A minute or so more and water began to spill across the spout and into the trough.

Longarm pumped the trough half-full, and with the last few draws he filled his water bag, replaced the cap on it, and set the cold and heavy bag aside. He rolled his shirtsleeves and picked up double handfuls of water to splash on his face and neck, while at the other end of the trough the horse drank its fill. Finally he helped himself to a long, satisfying drink—from the water bag, not the trough, where horse slobber and mouse shit floated on the surface—and stepped up onto the sorrel.

He sat there for a minute visualizing the lay of things. La Junta was down . . . that way. Which put Pueblo . . . there. Denver over . . . that way. And that would mean the Z Slash had to be along about, mmm, there. He hoped. He reined the sorrel toward the Z Slash—assuming the outfit was where he thought it might be—and gigged the gelding into a slow trot.

It was already close to sundown, and he could have stayed the night under a roof back at the shell of what once had been Tipton's, but he suspected the empty building would house a herd of hungry fleas after standing empty so long, and he had no desire to wake up in the morning with half his blood left and a whole lot of scratching to look forward to.

Better to move along instead. Longarm figured he would keep going until he either found a good spot to set up for the night or until he came across the Z Slash.

As it happened, he did not do either of those things.

Chapter 19

Longarm grunted, both in surprise and in satisfaction. He had just about despaired of finding a sheltered place to set up camp for the night, and there in the distance he could see a light. Two lights actually, one large, steady one and another smaller and moving. Unless the antelope hereabouts had figured out a way to make lamps, or at the very least fire, there pretty much had to be human folks up ahead. Longarm put the sorrel into a lope, relying on its eyesight, so much better than his own in the dark, to avoid any pitfalls.

The smaller of the two lights disappeared—a lantern, that one would almost surely be—while the big one remained constant. Five or so minutes later the little one reappeared going in the other direction. A very large rectangle of light showed itself and the little one disappeared into it. By that time Longarm was close enough to make out that the new, very large light was a doorway, and the little one was being carried by a dark shape against the brightly lighted door.

At the very least, Longarm figured he should be able to borrow the use of a straw pile overnight. That would be much more comfortable than laying out the sorrel's blanket on the hard, cold ground. After all, he left Denver expecting to take the rails to Cañon City, visit with Neal Bird, and then possibly go home, if he didn't take on Bird's case. He had not brought a bedroll or any other preparations for laying out under the stars. He could do it. Of course he could. But a farm shed would be way the hell better.

"Hello the house," Longarm called out loudly as he rode in past a pump and trough.

The door swung open, spilling lamplight across a small porch and onto the ground, and a dark shape stood in the doorway with what looked like a scattergun draped over the crook of an arm.

"Who are ye? What d'ye want?" a raspy voice called.

"Custis Long, deputy U.S. marshal outta Denver," he called back.

"You got proof o' that?"

"I do."

"What be your business here?"

"Just passing by. I'm hoping to to find a place to sleep tonight. Maybe a bite to eat for me and for this horse."

"I can't afford to feed every damn wandering Jew as comes by my door."

"I can pay."

"You a Jew?"

"No, why?" Longarm asked as he swung down off the sorrel.

"'Cause that's the saying but I never met none. I been kinda hoping to, one o' these days."

"Sorry. I can't accommodate you." He flipped his near stirrup over the seat of the old saddle and loosened the center-fire cinch strap. "Where would you like me to put this horse?"

"The corral yonder would be all right. There's hay in the bunk. He can eat his fill of that. It's sweet hay. No mold nor loco weed. Water's in the trough where he can get to it."

"All right, thanks." Longarm led the sorrel to the corral, felt his way along until he found the moveable gate rails, and let the animal inside before he pulled his gear—what little of it there was—and draped the saddle over the top fence rail.

The man with the shotgun stood silhouetted in the doorway watching him the whole time. Finally, when the horse was bedded down and Longarm approached the house, the man took a step back to where the light shined on him.

Except it was not a him but a her. The person with the shotgun and the rough voice was a short, stocky woman of forty or so with strands of gray in her hair. She wore a man's rugged work clothes. She moved aside to give Longarm room to enter. When he did, she looked him up and down as if inspecting a side of beef to decide if she wanted to buy.

"You'll do," she said.

"Well, I'm surely glad 'bout that," Longarm told her.

"You hungry?"

"I am."

"Set ye down. I'll put meat on the table."

"Thank you." He started to pull out a chair at the table and she said, "Not there. That one." She pointed to a spot on the opposite side of the table. Longarm noticed that the light from the wall lamps would shine brighter on that side. Apparently she wanted to examine him further. It had been a long day. He was tired. The bottom line was that he really did not give a shit. He took the chair she indicated.

"Side meat. Hominy. Fried taters. That fill you up?"

"It sounds like somebody has gone an' told you what my favorites are," Longarm said.

The woman grunted and went to her range. She opened the firebox and used an iron poker to stir the ashes until she found live coals, then added hay twists to get some flame and dried cow shit until she had a fire she liked.

The range must still have been hot from cooking her supper, because it did not take long to get her skillet and a cast iron pot hot enough for her liking. She rather noisily banged a tin plate and mug in front of Longarm, then added knife, fork, and spoon out of a pan sitting beside the dry sink.

Coffee was already in the pot, obviously leftover from her own meal and quite possibly what she had intended for herself come morning. She poured Longarm's mug too full to hold any canned milk. If he wanted milk. If there had been some, which there was not.

"I got no sugar," she said from the stove, where she was busy with a spider full of side meat. The pork smelled good enough that Longarm was tempted to grab a chunk and eat it whether it was cooked or not.

The coffee was good, though, if not yet very hot, and in the fullness of time Longarm had a right proper meal before him.

They had not broached the subject of payment, Longarm realized when he was almost finished polishing off everything that had been set in front of him and was thinking about asking for more.

Best to be polite, he decided. He did kind of wonder, though, what she intended to charge for all this.

When he was done eating, the woman piled his dirty dishes into a pail and set it beside the stove.

"You're tired," she said.

"Ayuh. I am."

"Sleep then. That bed there."

"That's your bed, isn't it?"

"It be," she agreed.

"I don't want to put you outta your own bed. D'you have a pallet I can lay out on the floor or something?"

"Hmm. Polite one, ain't you? Just you let me worry 'bout where I lay these old bones. You're a guest in this house. You'll sleep in the best bed." It appeared to be the only bed in the place too, but it would have been impolite for him to mention that. The old broad was obviously treating him as an honored guest, and it would have been boorish for him to refuse her hospitality.

"Thank you." It was about all he could say.

"Mind if I have me a pipe?" she asked. "I most gen'r'ly do about now."

"No, of course not. Do you mind if I smoke a cigar?"

"Go 'head. I ain't stopping ye." She opened the firebox and stuck a sliver of fat wood in, then brought it out and used it to light both Longarm's cheroot and her own pipe, before dropping what was left back into the flames and closing the firebox door.

The woman turned the lamps down, and the two of them sat in silence until eventually she decided that was long enough. She stood and laid her pipe aside, then said, "Take yer boots off afore ye crawls inta the bed." With that she turned and left. Went outside and disappeared into the night.

Going to the barn, Longarm supposed. If there was a barn. Or anyway probably heading for some place where she could stretch out and get some sleep.

Strange woman, he thought. But hospitable.

He wondered what she intended to charge for his board and the horse's.

He sat on the edge of the borrowed bed and removed his gunbelt, kicked his boots off, and lay down.

Chapter 20

Longarm was drifting comfortably toward sleep. The feeling was good. He was warm. He had food in his belly. A man could not ask for much more than . . . His eyes came open and his muscles tensed. The door latch lifted and the door faintly squealed on old hinges as it swung open.

Someone . . . He relaxed. The woman. It was only the woman coming back inside for the night. So she hadn't gone off to a barn or something. Fine. He was sure she knew what she was doing.

Shit! *He* would like to know what she was up to.

She came across the floor to stand over him where he lay on her bed.

She started taking her damn clothes off.

This was *not* a woman he particularly wanted to see naked. Not any more than he had any desire to see a heifer bare-ass naked. And the two were about the same weight. Damn woman was built like a whiskey barrel. Given the choice, though, Longarm would have preferred the whiskey barrel.

She stripped off until there wasn't a stitch on her. Not a

damn thing covering those rolls of fat and muscle. Nothing but hair. Which she had a gracious plenty of. Near covering her legs. Hanging out of her armpits. Even some long, dark hairs spiked atop her nipples, which themselves were as big as some women's thumbs. And she had a patch of cunt hair like a rug, thick and black and curly. Stinking too. He could smell it from where he lay, paralyzed by shock and fear.

She didn't expect . . . Surely she couldn't want. . . . Oh, shit!

She smiled. And straddled him, one chubby knee on either side of his waist, pinning him to the bed. Probably thought he wanted to escape. She'd be right about that if she did think so too.

One thing sure, it didn't matter what she wanted, his pecker was not likely to cooperate. No way could he get a hard-on while he was looking at that.

Damn woman raised her ass to make room for her hands so she could unbutton his britches.

She did not even bother to pull his trousers down, just reached inside, found the blind snake, and pulled it out.

There was more of a chill in the air than he had realized. Or maybe it was his imagination that made his prick feel so cold. And lonely.

Ah, dammit. Now that just wasn't fair. She was working him up and down, rubbing her hands on him, getting the treacherous, miserable, son of a bitch of a cock to betray him.

Who was the master here anyway?

Okay, so maybe it was.

Damn thing was rising from the dead in spite of his strenuous objections. Lifting and becoming hard. Standing tall against his explicit instruction that it should play possum.

Which he was certainly intent on doing.

Longarm stiffened. Closed his eyes. Felt the woman shift position a little and then felt the wet heat as she lowered herself onto him.

His disobedient pecker shoved its way deep inside the woman.

She lifted her butt. Jammed it down again. Over and over and endlessly—it seemed endless anyway—over again.

He could feel her shudder, and the grip of her cunt on his shaft tightened. She grabbed hold of his shoulders so hard he fretted that she might break bones in there.

She yelped—he could have sworn it sounded more like a bark than anything else—and began to quiver.

That was bad enough. Worse was when Longarm felt his own sap commence to rise. And then to burst out in a geyser of jism.

Lordy! He found himself clenching the blanket with both hands and trying to hold himself still.

He could not believe any of this was happening. Damn her anyway. She might have asked, for crying out loud, instead of just taking what she wanted. Might at the very least have considered his feelings about fucking.

Instead she just had her way with him. Now she dismounted, casual as could be, and used a piece of rag to wipe the juices off his cock. When she was done wiping him, she shoved the rag between her own legs. Then she very carefully tucked his now flaccid pecker back inside his britches and even took the time to button his fly back the way she found it.

"I like you," she said. "You're paid up for tonight. If you wanta stay longer you can. Good night now." She turned, gathered up her clothes, and left, going out into the night again. Longarm did not know where she went, but this time she stayed out there.

He closed his eyes and almost immediately slept.

Chapter 21

"Thanks for the breakfast, ma'am. An' . . . everything."

"You come back anytime, hear?"

"Yes, ma'am. Thank you." Truth was he was feeling pretty good this morning. Good night's sleep. Good shit first thing this morning. Good breakfast warm under his belt. And his ashes had been hauled. Not so much to his liking, perhaps, but thoroughly.

He went out to the corral and snapped a lead rope onto the sorrel's halter, tied it to a fence post, and saddled it. The woman sat watching from her porch. Longarm stepped onto the horse and nodded to her. He touched the brim of his hat and gigged the sorrel into a walk.

The Z Slash, she'd said, was southeast, so he tugged the brim of his Stetson low to keep the rising sun out of his eyes and pointed the horse toward the dawn. An hour and a half later he found a collection of buildings that suggested a sizeable ranching outfit.

A long, low building with a cold chimney at each end and a stovepipe streaming smoke close to the north end was most likely the cookhouse, Longarm thought. He rode to it, rather than the fine, three-story house that was at the center of things.

"Hello," he called loudly. "Anybody around?"

He called twice before the cookhouse door opened and a small, gray-haired man with a withered left arm stepped outside. "You can quit bellowin' now. Any chickens that wasn't awake before, you've sure as hell woke 'em by now."

"Just what I intended," Longarm said with a grin. He crossed his hands on the saddle horn and leaned on them, waiting.

"Well are you gonna step down or would you ruther just set there?" the cook demanded.

"The view's fine from up here and the saddle is comfortable enough but I'm thinking I smell coffee in there," Longarm told him.

"Then come in an' have some."

Longarm dismounted and tied the sorrel to a hitch ring screwed into the butt end of one of the logs the place was made of. He followed the cook inside.

"Coffee's in the pot yonder. Cups is over there. There's fixings on the table. Help yourself to whatever you like, an' if you're hungry I could maybe find some leftover ham and eggs and biscuits and such. An' if you're looking for work, well, you ain't dressed like a cowpuncher but the outfit is shorthanded. Likely you could hook on here."

"That's good of you, Coosie, but I already got a job." Longarm introduced himself.

"Federal, eh? That's some serious shit."

Longarm picked a cup, filled it, and stirred in some brown sugar and canned cow.

"You looking for one of our boys?"

"Just to talk to, I am. I hear the man might know some stuff I need to find out from him."

"An' who would this fella be?"

"There's two of them actually. One is Zenas Perch. The other," Longarm shrugged, "all I know is that he's called Billy Boy."

"That bein' the case, Marshal, you're here about Neal Bird, ain't you?"

"Yes, sir, so I be."

"He ain't hung yet?"

"Not for another week or so," Longarm told him. "I'm here to verify the facts of the case before he drops."

"I can help you with the one of those boys," the cook said. "Perch, he came back here after the trial . . . Him and Billy was both subpoenaed for the trial, you know . . . He's out in one o' the line camps now. I dunno which one, but Lew can tell you."

"Lew?"

"Lewis Bonwit. He's the foreman here."

Longarm nodded. "All right, I'll talk to him. What about Billy Boy?"

The cook smiled just a little. "Might surprise you, but I think his name really is Billy Boy. Except it's spelled b-u-o-y. You know. Buoy. Like one of them things that floats in the water."

"Billy Buoy." Longarm grunted. "Makes sense. Sort of."

"Anyway, Buoy went off to the trial. He never came back."

"He never testified either," Longarm said. "He never showed up at the trial. His lawyers said they couldn't find him."

"Then they're lying sons o' bitches," the cook said. "A

paperhanger showed up here with the subpoenas for the
both of them, just like I told you. I know that for a fact
because he sat right where you are an' gave them to me to
read so I could point him at the right fellas. He waited till
suppertime an' served his papers right in this very room. I
seen it done."

"You seem to know a lot about subpoenas and such,"
Longarm said. "Ever worn a badge yourself?"

The cook broke into a wide grin. "Is it obvious?"

"Maybe not to an ordinary hand but it is to another
lawman. Where was it?"

"Over in Kansas. I was night constable in Wichita for a
spell and town marshal a couple other places. Little burgs,
like. Then some sorry son of a bitch running a still came
at me. I was busting up his jugs o' whiskey. Costing him
his profits. He picked up an axe an' tried to take my head
off with it. I flung my arm up against the blow and've
never been the same since. So I learned to cook." He
smiled. "It's a wonder these boys out here didn't die of
the bellyache before I got onto the hang of it."

"I don't know about your cooking, but you've sure as
hell learned to make coffee. Mind if I have a refill?"

"You help yourself to whatever you want, deputy. If
you should get hungry afore the foreman comes in just tell
me. I can fry you up a steak just any way you want it."

"That's mighty kind of you, Coosie."

"If you don't mind, Marshal, I know every cook this
side o' the Mississippi is called Coosie. Maybe the other
side of it too for all I know. But . . . my real name is Harold Ware. I'd be real proud if you was to use it."

Longarm reached over and offered his hand to shake.
"Mr. Ware, it's a pleasure knowin' you."

"Set down, Marshal . . ."

"Longarm to my friends," Longarm said. "It would please me for you to call me that."

Ware smiled his appreciation of the offer and said, "Set and relax, Longarm. First thing Lew always does when he gets back is to come in here for a cup o' coffee before he goes over an' does his business with the big boss. I'll be sure you meet him, quick as he walks through that door over there."

"Thank you, Mr. Ware."

"Harold to my friends, Longarm."

Chapter 22

Lew Bonwit was a stocky man, younger than Longarm would have expected. What he lacked in years he made up for in mustache. Bonwit's 'stache put Longarm's to shame. It was thick enough you could hide a good-sized calf in it. It probably required a quart of beeswax just to hold it firm against the wind. If he really put his mind to mustache raising, Longarm thought, Bonwit could grow his until he could drape it over his ears and down his back. Damn, but Longarm envied the man that mustache.

He told Bonwit so.

The Z Slash foreman laughed until his belly hurt. "Are you *sure* I can't tempt you to change jobs?" Bonwit asked. "You'd be good to have around." He looked at Harold Ware and added, "Ain't that the truth, Coosie."

"It sure as hell is, Lew." To Longarm he said, "I thought you two might hit it off pretty good. Longarm is here, Lew, looking into the Tipton murder that Neal Bird is fixing to swing for."

Bonwit raised an eyebrow at that news. "Bird? I thought he'd hung already."

"Not yet," Longarm told him. "You knew him, of course. What did you think of him?"

"The boy seemed a steady enough hand. When it came time to lay boys off for the winter, I'd've liked to hang onto Bird. That's the only way to be sure a man will be here for the spring workings, you know. They come and they go, these mangy cowhands, and you just can't carry them all over the winter. After what happened, though, I wisht all the more that I'd been able to keep Bird. I liked that boy."

"And Zenas Perch and Bill Buoy, did you like them too?"

"Wait just a minute here, Long, while I get me a cup of Coosie's horse liniment." He stood and walked over to the side table where the cups and coffeepot were. Coosie went with him, poured coffee for the foreman, and then disappeared into the kitchen, leaving Longarm alone with Bonwit. "Another for you, Marshal?" the foreman asked when he returned to the table where the three men had been sitting.

"I'm fine for now," Longarm said, "but I thank you." He took a sip from his cup and said, "You were about to tell me about Zenas Perch an' Billy Buoy, what kinda hands they were and what you thought of them."

"Oh, I haven't forgot. Just trying to get my thoughts in order here. Let me put it this way. I'm pleased to have Perch back in the outfit this year, and I'm just as pleased that I don't have Billy Boy."

"Why's that, Mr. Bonwit?"

Bonwit stared off into the distance for a moment before he answered. "Mind you, Billy never gave us no trouble. Not really. But there was ... Somehow, Marshal, I was always expecting that he would. Like he was walking the sharp edge of a knife blade and you never were sure which side he might fall on if he was to topple. Do you know what I mean? He was a powder keg just looking for a spark. None came that I ever saw. But that doesn't mean there wasn't any danger in him."

"Was he a gunslick?"

Bonwit shook his head. "No, sir, he wasn't. Not fascinated with guns the way some bad ones seem to be. Nor a brawler. Billy wasn't one to pick fights in the bunkhouse nor hold grudges toward others. But there was just . . . something. I don't know what, exactly. Don't know how to explain it so you can understand, Marshal."

"Oh, I think you already have. You didn't like him, did you? Didn't trust him."

"Not half as far as I could throw him," Bonwit said.

"Zenas Perch," Longarm said. "I'll be wanting to talk to him."

"He won't be in for another week and a half, Marshal. That's when I'll be relieving the boys at our north camp. They're up there trying to keep John Seidman's beeves from coming down and eating our grass."

Longarm smiled. "And south o' you there's some other outfit's line camp trying to keep Z Slash beef from drifting with the wind."

Bonwit chuckled. And nodded. "Yes, sir, that's true too. You want to wait for Perch? You're welcome to stay here. Lord knows, we got bunks open that ought to be filled this time of year."

"Thanks, but I'll go to him. Neal Bird is fixing to hang in just a week or so. I can't wait around." He smiled. "Though I'd like to if Mr. Ware has learned to cook as good as he can make coffee. As it is, Mr. Bonwit, I'd appreciate it if you was to point me toward this north camp o' yours."

The foreman nodded. "Might be easier, then, if I was to guide you out there myself. It's easy to ride clean past it if you don't know what you're looking for."

"I didn't come here to disturb your routine, Mr. Bonwit, but your offer sounds fine to me."

"I'll need to go over to the house and tell the boss where I'm going. We can leave in the morning."

Longarm dragged his bulb-shaped, railroad-grade Ingersoll out of his pocket and consulted it for the time. "Can't we leave this afternoon? We could get a good three, four hours in before dark."

Bonwit grunted once, then quickly stood. "All right. I'll go tell the boss and be right back." He raised his voice. "Coosie, pack us up some eatables to carry with us. Enough for tonight and tomorrow morning too." To Longarm he said, "Fifteen minutes. Will that be all right with you?"

Longarm nodded. "I'll be ready."

Bonwit hurried outside. Longarm ambled over to the table and got himself a last half cup of coffee.

Chapter 23

Longarm reined his horse to a halt beside Lew Bonwit's tall, fast-moving Tennessee walker.

"We'll take a breather here. Be at the line shack in time for noon dinner," Bonwit said.

Longarm sent a suspicious look skyward. The sun was very near its zenith and there was no sign of a line shack or any other form of human habitation. "Noon," he repeated, the skepticism plain in his voice.

"I said it and I meant it," Bonwit confirmed with a smile. He raised one arm and pointed down off the hill where they sat. "See that bottom?"

"Sure I do," Longarm said. The wrinkle in the earth lay ahead of and slightly below them. It held the usual trickle of water, hint of grass, and scant growth of brush.

"That's the line camp down there," Bonwit said.

"I don't see anything."

"Look close again. On the west side of that little vale is a dugout. I helped build it myself some years back when I was just a hand here. There was some timber in the bottom then. Aspen. We cut it and used it for roof poles and to line the walls. There's three feet of dirt over top of those poles, and we cut sod and laid it in place so it would grow and hold everything together. The littlest piece of fire will keep that place warm and comfortable as your mama's bosom," the foreman said, obviously pleased with the work he and some other boys had accomplished years earlier.

"How come I don't see any smoke now?" Longarm asked.

"Why, that's because there's no fire at the moment. At least there damn well better not be. If I was to find those boys laying out in their bunks when they're supposed to be riding line, I'd fire their asses on the spot. And they know it. No, they'll be out somewhere earning their pay. Won't be back until dark or thereabouts."

"But . . . but," Longarm stammered, "if that's the case, why the hell are we settin' here now? Why'd we come so early?"

"Mister Deputy, yesterday you told me you wanted to get some hours of riding in before dark. Reckon we did that too. Made good time and now we're here early enough we can go down and make ourselves some dinner, then set and tell lies until Zenas Perch and Tommy Haggin come in this evening."

Bonwit's face cracked into a huge grin. He tossed his head back so it was a wonder his hat didn't fall off, and he set to laughing like he had pulled the best stunt ever. Longarm suspected the foreman would be telling this story for years to come, with one Deputy United States Marshal Custis Long as the butt of the thing.

It was a good one, though, making the both of them sleep outside on the cold, cold ground when they could have enjoyed Harold Ware's cooking—which could not possibly be any worse than Lew Bonwit's had been—and slept on soft mattresses last night.

"Y'know, Mr. Bonwit, if I was to work at it, I could manage to take an intense dislike to you," Longarm said. But he was laughing when he said it.

"Come along, Mr. Long. We'll go down and see if there's any coffee in the pot or do we have to make some fresh."

"This," Longarm announced, "is just almost exactly what I would imagine a boar hog's nest to smell like."

"That's honest sweat you're smelling," Bonwit told him.

"Or the leavings of a family of skunks."

Bonwit grinned and shrugged. "Yeah, that too maybe. Leave that door propped open a bit so I can have enough light to find the lamp. Ah. There. Got it, thanks." The foreman struck a match and touched it to the wick of a kerosene lamp that hung suspended from the ceiling.

Sheets of once white, now yellow muslin had been tacked to the roof poles to catch any dirt that filtered down off the sod above. There were two bunks pegged into the back corners of the single ten-by-ten room and between them against the back wall was a folding, sheet-metal sheepherder's stove. A fire had been laid in it ready to light when the riders got in at the end of their day. A stout table, factory-made but also collapsible, sat in the middle of the floor with a homemade three-legged stool on each side of it. A deck of greasy cards and a checkerboard were the entertainments.

"Ever see anything like it?" Bonwit asked.

"Friend, I've wintered in worse than this."

The foreman raised an eyebrow.

"Up in Nebraska one year," Longarm told him. "I was a young buck. Figured I could take on anything. Hired out

to a man and found out too late that he didn't believe in
wasting time or money on anything as low-down as a
waddie. The line shack would've made this place seem a
palace, and he fed even worse than he bedded. But I
learned a lot that winter so I've no regrets."

"You worked cows then?"

Longarm nodded. "Some. I've done most everything,
one time or another. Everything short of murder for hire
anyway."

"You like the lawing business?" Bonwit asked.

"I do. Let's me feel like maybe I'm doing somebody
some good." He straddled one of the stools, cautiously at
first until he tested its steadiness, and reached for a cheroot. He nipped off the twist with his teeth and spat it into
his palm, stuck the thin cigar between his teeth and leaned
forward to the lamp that was suspended low over the
table.

"When your riders get in," he said, "I'd appreciate it if
you'd make the introductions, then if you don't mind I'll
take Perch aside for a little private talk. I've found that I
can read a man better if there's no distractions. No others
thinking to join in the conversation. I don't mean to be
rude, mind you. I'm just trying to get things straight."

"You think there's a chance Neal didn't do what he's
fixing to hang for?" Bonwit asked.

"Ask me that again when we're on our way back to the
Z Slash come tomorrow morning. Mayhap I'll have an
answer for you then." Longarm puffed on his cheroot.
And waited.

Chapter 24

Zenas Perch proved to be a tall, skinny kid—kid from Longarm's vantage point anyway—in his early twenties or thereabouts. He was quiet and friendly. Longarm suspected Perch was honest, as a great many untutored country boys are. After Lew Bonwit completed the requisite introduction, Longarm took Perch by the elbow and said, "Let's us walk out an' see to the horses."

Perch looked nervous. He made no attempt to pull away, but it was clear he did not want to go. Longarm could feel Perch's body stiffen, and for a moment he thought the young man might refuse to go with him, but after five or ten seconds had passed, Perch sighed and held his hands out toward Longarm. He pulled his shirtsleeves back and stood there waiting.

"What the hell is that for?" Longarm asked, peering down at Perch's wrists and forearms.

"Aren't you gonna put handcuffs on me?"

"Why would I do that?"

"Isn't that what you're here for? To arrest me?" He continued to stand there with his wrists bared, ready for the irons.

"No," Longarm said. "Have you done anything to be arrested *for*?"

"No, sir, I reckon not. Not that I know of anyhow."

"Not that I know of neither. I just want to talk to you."

"Oh, I . . . I thought . . ."

"Yeah, so I see. No, but what I want to talk to you about I'd rather it be in private. I want you to be able to say any damn thing and it not come back to bite you, no matter what. What I'm wanting from you is some truth."

"All right, sir. Uh . . . sorry 'bout, well, you know."

"Sure. Don't worry about it." Longarm led the way outside and about fifty yards away, to a grassy spot high on the east bank of the little draw where the line camp was situated. He settled cross-legged onto the ground there and motioned for Perch to join him. The horses, hobbled and turned loose on the grass, were below them and about a hundred yards out. A quarter mile or so farther a small herd of pronghorn antelope grazed, their black-and-white rump patches bright in the last slanting rays of the day's sunshine.

"Did you mean it in there, Deputy? Am I really not in trouble?"

"Truth is, son, I'm not real sure yet." But he thought he knew. Longarm did not think he was speaking with a killer in Zenas Perch.

"What, uh . . . ?"

"I want to talk with you about Neal Bird. You remember him, don't you?"

"Yes, sir, of course. He been hanged yet?"

"No. Will be real soon though. What I'm doin' is checking up. It's something we always do at the last minute," Longarm lied, "whenever there's to be an execution. It ain't easy to apologize to a dead man, and we don't like to make mistakes when it comes to hanging offenses." He figured if he put it like that and Zenas Perch himself was guilty of the murder—which Longarm did not for a minute suspect now that he'd met the kid—Perch would be quick to start digging Bird's grave.

"That makes sense," Perch agreed. "So what do you want to know?"

"Everything you can remember about that day at Tipton's store."

"Have you heard Neal's side of it?" Perch asked.

"No. All I done was to bring him in. And of course I seen him across the room during the trial, what of it I bothered to listen to back then. Now I been ordered to look into it again, as a last resort sort o'fthing, and that's why I need to talk to you. I need to hear your side of the story."

"What of it I can remember," Perch said. "Truth is, Marshal, I was awful drunk that evening."

"Whatever you can remember, son. Everything of it, including about that Injun girl."

"Yes, sir. Well what of it I can recall . . ."

Perch told very much the same story that Neal Bird had, right down to the order in which the three laid-off hands used the girl. "It was terrible what happened to her, Marshal. I saw her body afterward, and I mean, I wouldn't treat a hog the way she was tore up. That was ugly. Real ugly. But what all happened that day I just surely don't know. I remember I fucked the girl at least twice. So did Neal. And Billy, he took her twice. Maybe more often. I wouldn't know about that. I remember I got sick and passed out. I guess it was Neal that discovered the bodies, then he woke me up."

"Billy was gone by then?" Longarm asked.

Perch nodded. "Yes, sir, he was. I never knew where he went nor why."

"You testified at Bird's trial, didn't you?"

"Yes, sir. What little I could recall. Not that it made much difference. I got the idea that jury had their minds made up before Neal or anybody else said a word to them. I even noticed a couple of them dozing off during the trial."

"The judge didn't do anything about that?"

"No, sir. I know he saw them but he never said a word. Didn't try and wake them up either." Perch shook his head. "I hadn't known that trials can be so strung out and boring as that one was. The only person that seemed to be paying close attention, other than me I mean, was Neal. I could see he was awful bad worried. Turns out he had pretty good reason to be."

"I'm going to want to talk with Billy Buoy, Zenas. Any idea where I might could find him?"

"Billy a couple times mentioned a girlfriend, had a whorehouse down around Trinidad or . . . no, I think it was for sure in Trinidad."

Longarm grunted. "That's a shame. Whores move around even more than cowhands do."

"No, Marshal, maybe it was just Billy bragging on her, but I think she used to *own* this whorehouse. Of course Billy might've been lying through his teeth when he said that stuff, but I'm pretty sure I remember him saying it."

Longarm stood, his knee joints crackling. Perch's story was almost exactly the same as Bird's. Corroborated it completely. But it did nothing to disprove Bird's guilt. It only confirmed that Zenas Perch had been passed out in a drunken stupor when Tipton and the girl were killed.

"Neal was a pretty good old boy," Perch mused, staring out over the grassy plains. "A pretty good old boy."

"If I see him again I'll tell him you said so," Longarm offered. He walked out to the horses and retrieved his. It was late, but he intended to set out again immediately after supper. He did not know how much more time Neal Bird had before that dressed oak trapdoor dropped out from under his feet. He could strike straight south, he figured, and hit the railroad somewhere between La Junta and the Colorado-Kansas state line.

Chapter 25

"He do all right for you?" the liveryman asked when Longarm dismounted and led the sorrel into the barn.

Longarm nodded. "Did just fine, thanks."

He flipped the near stirrup over the saddle seat and loosened the cinch, then pulled the saddle and blanket. "Where d'you want these, mister?"

"On that rack over there. I'll clean 'em up later." He smiled. "No offense to you, but not everybody treats things the way I do. Generally speaking, I find it's better to do things myself than to get mad at the other fella for not doing it my way."

Longarm smiled his appreciation of the attitude. He and the hostler, one working on either side of the horse, began currying, brushing, cleaning the feet of the animal.

"Mind if I ask you something?" Longarm said as he bent over to use a dandy brush on the sorrel's lower legs.

"You just did," the liveryman said with a chuckle.

"All right. Mind if I ask you something else?"

"Shoot."

"What's the best way to get down to Trinidad?"

"Depends on what you mean by 'best.' Now to me,

best would be the prettiest country and cheerfullest folks along the way. But then I'm not generally in much of a hurry to get any place. So to me, the best way to go would be to put the saddle back onto this here horse and head him southwest. Hit the Picketwire and follow it upstream until you come to Trinidad."

"And the quickest?"

The liveryman grunted. "Get back onto that smelly railroad coach and change to a southbound once you get to Pueblo."

"Thanks. I suspected that but wanted to hear it from you before I went back over to the depot. Any idea when the next westbound is due through?"

"No idear at all."

"I do thank you. You been mighty helpful, friend. How much would you say I owe you now?"

Longarm settled his bill with cash out of pocket but asked for a receipt. If Neal Bird's claim proved out, Longarm expected he would put in a voucher for reimbursement of expenses. If it *didn't* pan out, he would soon have to start traveling on the strength of his badge and reimburse the government later on. And wouldn't Henry have a time figuring out how to go about such a transaction. Hell, nobody ever paid the government back for anything.

He picked up his bag and headed for the railroad station, wishing he could do something . . . anything . . . to get this over and done with. Neal Bird had mighty little time left, and Custis Long did not want to be responsible for the death of an innocent man. Even worse, he did not want to be the one to let a guilty man go free.

Chapter 26

It was an hour or more short of daybreak when the Santa Fe train pulled into Pueblo. Longarm came to his feet with a yawn and a grimace. Hours spent being jostled back and forth on an unpadded railcar bench had left him with grit in his eyes and a vile taste in his mouth. What he needed was about ten hours of sound sleep. In a bed. That did not move and bump and shake. What he could expect to get was . . . not damned much.

He stretched and stamped his feet and tried to work some circulation into his limbs. He felt of his face and found it to be as scratchy as his eyes felt. After that sleep that he was not going to get, he thought, he needed a shave that would not likely happen either.

A conductor, who looked to be as weary as Longarm felt, appeared at the front of the car.

"All out for Pueblo. Pueblo, Colorado. All out for Pueblo."

"Excuse me, neighbor. Can you tell me when the next southbound is due through?"

"Sorry, sir. That's on the Denver and Rio Grande line. I don't know what their schedule would be."

"All right. Thanks." Longarm yawned again and picked up his carpetbag. He made his way to the front of the car, past the few other bleary-eyed passengers, and stepped down onto the platform. The night air was chill after the closeness of the passenger coach. It smelled of coal smoke and cinders. Longarm shivered and pulled his coat tighter around his torso. The gesture did no good, but it made him feel a little better for having tried.

Only two others detrained in Pueblo. They took their bags and quickly disappeared into the night.

The timing of his arrival left Longarm with a dilemma. Should he lay over long enough to see Hank Bayles about the legal effort to delay the execution? Or should he go straight to the D&RG depot to make sure he was on the first available southbound to Trinidad?

"Need a hansom, sir?" a voice called from the darkness. "Transfer to the other station perhaps?"

Longarm hesitated only a moment. "Yes. Yes, I need to transfer." At the D&RG station he could at least find out when there was a southbound coming through. It could be there would be time enough for him to see Hank Bayles and still make the next available train to Trinidad. If not . . . he would think about it once he knew for sure. "Yes. Coming," he said in a louder voice.

He left the platform and found the cab, a dark shape in the night, and opened the door to toss his bag in. He felt the cab sway on its leathers as the driver moved around on his perch above.

"If you're headed north," the man said, "you've no problem, sir, as that train won't be leaving till eight-thirty, but if you're headed south, you'd best tell me and I can get a move on lest you miss it. We've just enough time to make that one."

"South it is," Longarm called up to him.

"Then hurry in, sir, and I'll see can old Tim get you there in time."

Longarm was not sure if the horse was named Tim or if that would be the driver, but whoever it was, he indeed hoped they got to the D&RG depot in time for him to make the Trinidad connection.

He slammed the hansom door closed and almost instantly heard the crack of the driver's whip. The coach lurched forward, rocking on its leather springs, and the horse—Tim?—quickly picked up into a trot.

At least, Longarm thought, that answered his question whether he should try to see Bayles first or take the next available train south. It seemed the railroad's schedule was deciding that for him.

Longarm reached inside his coat for a cheroot and into his vest for a match to light it. The cigar, he knew, would not remove the foul flavor in his mouth, but with luck it might paper over it. Then when he got to Trinidad he could find a café and buy himself a proper breakfast. That should do the trick.

And when that was taken care of all he had to do was to find this woman who owned a whorehouse and who was sweet on Billy Buoy.

That shouldn't take long. After all, how many whorehouses could there be in a tiny burg like Trinidad?

Chapter 27

It was the middle of a clear and sunny afternoon when Longarm stepped off the Denver and Rio Grande coach onto the platform outside Trinidad. The railyard was cluttered with coal cars and loading chutes, making it clear to anyone who cared to look that this was a working man's station and not for Sunday tourists.

"Cab, mister?" a man wearing a top hat and a shabby black cutaway called from atop a hansom. His horse, a dull brown animal whose ribs showed plain, was as ill kempt as the driver. Its owner was thin to the point of being skeletal. He needed a shave. For that matter, so did the horse.

Longarm glanced east from the railyard. The town of Trinidad was not but a few hundred yards distant, and he was a man who did not mind walking. Usually. "How much to the town marshal's office?" he asked, tipping his head back and holding onto his hat against the breeze that swirled down from the peaks that lay to the west.

"That'd be only a quarter, mister."

"All right, a quarter it is." Longarm opened the door of the hansom and tossed his bag in, then followed it and settled onto the cracked leather of the rear seat. "I'm set," he called as he pulled the door closed.

The rig eased forward with not a hint of a lurch. Perhaps there was something to be said for decrepit animals, he thought; they were too damned worn out and road weary to make any sudden moves.

They rolled across two sets of tracks and onto Trinidad's main street. The town was much busier than the last time Longarm had been there, but then the once sleepy cow town had been added to by coal miners in from the nearby diggings and by D&RG construction crews who were struggling to force the rails south through Raton Pass into northern New Mexico. Longarm guessed there were twice as many saloons operating in town since his last visit. Probably that many more whorehouses too.

"Here you are, mister," the driver shouted down from his box high on the front of the hansom. The rig rolled to a gentle halt and waited while Longarm collected his bag and crawled out. He handed the man three dimes and waved away the offer of change.

"Thank you, sir. The marshal's office is over there in that brown building."

Longarm touched the brim of his hat by way of acknowledgment and crossed the street to the two-story brown structure, part adobe and part lumber. He found the door he wanted and went in.

"Hello. Is John Howard in?" he asked of the pinch-faced little squirt who seemed to be the only one around.

"John don't work here anymore."

"How about Marshal Hammond?" He had worked with both Howard and Fred Hammond in the past.

"Him neither."

"Well, shit. Who does work here nowadays?"

"Me. And I'll thank you t'watch your fucking language an' your manners or I'll throw your ass in jail just for the pure pleasure of it." The scrawny little piece of shit leaned back in his swivel chair and turned to display the circular steel badge that was pinned to his vest. "Now, what is it you want, mister? Speak up, dammit, speak up."

"I, uh . . . I was just looking for the old marshal an' his deputy," Longarm said.

"They're around here somewheres," the new man said. From where he stood Longarm could not see the engraving on the badge to tell whether this asshole was the new town marshal or just a deputy. Either way, Longarm was not inclined to trust him to help. If Billy Buoy was in Trinidad, Longarm did not want him tipped off so he could run before Longarm got a chance to talk to him.

"Thanks then," Longarm said, backing out of the marshal's office and turning in the direction of a boarding-house he remembered from past visits to the town.

Lordy, he hoped that had not changed. The woman who ran it was a real piece of work. Old and ugly and full of complaints. She also had a heart as big as all of Colorado with half of New Mexico thrown in for good measure.

He hefted his bag and started walking east along the course of the Picketwire. If one insisted on calling such a slender trickle of water a river, that's what it was. The farther he went, the farther he got from the loud and often belligerent voices of the coal miners and gandy dancers, and the closer to the environs favored by cowhands and goatherds.

What he needed now was a room, some sleep, and William damn Buoy.

Chapter 28

Longarm removed his hat and did his best to appear respectful and inoffensive and decent. "Just for a night or two, ma'am," he said to the lady in the doorway. "I'm passing through on business and I need me a place to stay while I'm here. I'm a quiet sort. You'll hardly know I'm around."

The landlady gave him a skeptical look and a snort. "Dollar a night," she said. "In advance."

"Yes, ma'am." He dug into his pockets and came up with the required cash—Lordy, it was just killing him to be working without government expenses to fall back on—and handed it over. "That's for the two nights. If I figure to stay any longer, I'll be sure and pay you more."

"All right then. Come inside. I'll show you to your room." The woman was something short of five feet tall but round as a whiskey barrel. Her gray hair was pulled back into a severe bun. She gave the lie to the old myth about fat people being jolly, for this one looked about as jolly as a Baptist preacher with a toothache. Longarm resolved to walk easy around her lest she whack him on the head with a spoon.

On the other hand, the delicious aromas drifting out of the kitchen suggested that she knew the proper uses for that spoon she had in her hand. Living on the cheese sandwiches available on railroad cars was making Longarm a pushover for home cooking.

"I'm Mrs. Garza."

"I'm, uh, Jones, ma'am. John Jones."

"All right, Mr. Jones. If you say so. This is your room. Be in by ten o'clock. That's when I lock the door."

"Yes, ma'am." The room was tiny and tidy and clean. An open window suggested Longarm could come and go at any hour if he really wanted to. He put his bag down on the foot of the sagging bed, turned, and asked, "Could you direct me to a close-by café please, Mrs. Garza. The smell of whatever you're cooking has me so hungry I might could grab that pillow and swallow it down."

The woman's scowling expression softened into a pleased smile. "Are you hungry, Mr. Jones? Come. Sit down. That's chicken and dumplings you're smelling now. And for dessert I have some gooseberry cobbler left over from last night. Sit down. That's right. Let me bring you a wee bite to eat."

The lady's "wee bite" proved to be enough food to overload a battleship. Or to get Custis Long's belly to groaning, also from overloading.

"Mrs. Garza, you are a paragon among women," Longarm declared when he finally admitted he could hold absolutely not another mouthful. He smiled. "And a heckuva fine cook. Thank you, ma'am. Now if you will excuse me . . ." He carefully folded his napkin and laid it beside his plate.

"Supper is promptly at six, Mr. Jones."

"And I shall be here for it, Mrs. Garza." The lady beamed with pleasure.

Time now, though, to get serious, Longarm thought as he went back to his room and removed his coat, vest, and string tie. He rolled his sleeves up and took a look at himself in the mirror. This would do, he decided. He let himself out onto the front porch and into the street.

Time now to give some thought to Billy Buoy and what he might know about the day Jason Tipton died.

Chapter 29

Longarm laid a quarter on the bar. "Shot and a beer," he said. The barkeep nodded and transferred Longarm's quarter into his money box before he moved to comply with the request. Longarm picked up the shot and raised it high. "To your good health," he said and downed the whiskey. It was as bad as he had feared, raw and without flavor.

"Another?" the barman asked.

Longarm shook his head and took a swallow of the beer to wash the taste of the whiskey out of his mouth. It, at least, was better than the whiskey had been. He reached for one of his cheroots, then remembered that they were in his coat pocket. And the coat was back in the rooming house. "What do you have for cigars?" he asked.

The barkeep pointed to three boxes sitting open beneath the backbar mirror. "Take your pick."

Longarm took his time looking them over, then said, "Let me see that box of crooks."

The bartender set the cedarwood box onto the bar beside Longarm's beer.

"Rum-soaked?"

"These is brandy crooks."

"I'll try one."

"Two cents." The barman picked up Longarm's nickel and returned three pennies and a pair of kitchen matches.

Longarm bit the twist off the end of the crook, scratched the match aflame, and lit his cigar. It was not good, but it was not horrid either. He exhaled a cloud of blue smoke and in a low voice said, "I'm looking for a fella. Maybe you know him."

"Oh, I don't know many folks," the barkeep said. He started to turn away.

"Wait. Please."

The bartender stopped. "Mister, I don't like to get mixed into other folks' affairs."

"But you like to be helpful maybe," Longarm said.

The barman grunted. But he stayed where he was, listening, if reluctantly.

"I got a message to deliver to a man. Fella is said to spend his time here. Like I said, could be that you know him. He goes by the name of Billy Boy."

"And how do you know him, mister?"

Longarm puffed on his cigar before answering. "Friend, I don't know the man. For all I know, you could be him. Like I said, I got a message for him."

"Important?"

"Not to me. It don't mean shit as far as I'm concerned, but I reckon it'd mean considerable to him."

"What's the message?"

"Are you him?"

"No, but I could pass the message on to him if I see him."

"Thanks, but this is for him alone."

"Can you tell me who it's from?"

Longarm drank down the last of his beer. "Nope."

"I'm just trying to be helpful," the barman said.

Longarm nodded. "Yeah. So am I." He sighed. "Thanks for the beer and the shot. And if you happen to run into this Billy Boy, tell him I'm in town looking for him."

"Will you be here long?"

"Couple days maybe." Longarm nodded and touched the brim of his hat, then turned and left, heading for the next saloon down the line.

Chapter 30

Once he'd left his message in a good cross-section of the saloons in town—the best among them and the worst, concentrating on those down at the cowhands' end of town—Longarm figured he should do the same with the whorehouses. But which?

If Billy Buoy really did have a madam for a girlfriend, he might well stick with her. And the girlfriend's girls if she was not the jealous type.

On the other hand, Buoy might like a little variety about such things but not want the girlfriend to know. Longarm simply did not know enough about the man to guess which way he might go, fidelity to the madam or playing butterfly among all of Trinidad's available whores.

And for that matter, Billy Buoy's whorehouse madam girlfriend could well be nothing more than a bunkhouse lie. The things a man says when he is in a cow camp forty miles from the nearest human female . . . well, those tales should not be held against him once payday comes.

The safest course, Longarm figured, would be to spread the word among the town's whores too.

He was acutely conscious of the fact that every passing hour brought Neal Bird closer to a meeting with Bob Conrad, that hangman from Leavenworth. And if there was a chance, any chance at all, that an innocent man could hang for another's crimes ... that was a notion that twisted Longarm's gut.

He tugged open the gate of a nicely tended house at the eastern edge of town, glanced at the red lamp burning in an upstairs window, and strode up the walk and onto the front porch.

A young black woman wearing a footman's livery opened the door to his knock. The cutaway coat was several sizes too large for her and the white knee-high stockings sagged, but the overall effect was fancy enough. "Suh," she said and greeted him with a smile. "Welcome."

"Thank you, little miss." Longarm stepped inside and removed his hat, which the girl promptly took from him.

"What is yo' preference, suh?"

"I've never been here before, miss. I expect I'd like to look around a bit first."

"Of course, suh. Please come this way." She led him into a large parlor filled with small groupings of furnishings. The centerpiece of each was a sort of settee but shorter than most, just a little wider than a deeply upholstered armchair. Call it wide enough for one and a half occupants. Longarm hid a small smile. The place was not exactly subtle, enforcing a closeness between visitors and whichever girl they might choose to sit with.

The primary colors in the room were pale blues and light cream. The walls were covered with flocked paper.

An upright player piano dominated one end of the room and a large fireplace the other. Lamps burned brightly throughout.

Longarm's attention was mostly focused on the girls, however. There were six present in the room when he arrived. They wore gowns that promised much but revealed little. Their gowns were muted pastel colors, not at all garish.

The girls were all gathered around a Parcheesi board set close to the fireplace. They paused in their conversations to look him over, but no one rushed to claim his business, giving the customer time to examine the merchandise and make a selection from among them.

There was nothing at all wrong with the wares being put on offer here, Longarm saw. The girls were all reasonably young, ranging from perhaps twenty into their thirties. All reasonably attractive. A nice selection of blondes and brunettes. A man would have to be very picky indeed to find nothing here to whet his interest.

"Would you like something to drink first?" the little black girl offered.

"No, I . . . I think I'd like to talk with the boss." This house, Longarm realized, would be for cattlemen, ranch owners, and perhaps the more settled foremen, with some more prosperous businessmen thrown in as well. But this was *not* a house where ordinary cowhands like Billy Buoy would go to get laid.

Here it likely would cost five or even ten dollars to crawl between the legs of one of these fillies. A working stiff was more likely to pay fifty cents to perhaps as much as a dollar to get his ashes hauled. And even if he had the money, it was questionable whether he would be welcomed here.

"This way, sir." The girl was brisk and businesslike now, not at all the purring, fawning little thing she had been to begin with. "Wait here," she said once she got him back into the foyer.

The girl disappeared into the back of the house and Longarm peeped into the parlor again. In a way it was a shame he wouldn't do any good here—at least not in any way that was apt to help Neal Bird—because two of those girls in there were quite stunning. The brunette in the lime green dress, for instance. And that blonde in the powder blue . . .

"Yes?"

This madam was not very likely to be Billy Buoy's girlfriend, Longarm saw. Not unless he fancied elderly women with rolls of fat hanging where their chin should be and tits that got lost above a belly big enough to scald hogs in.

Even so, Longarm smiled and nodded and told the woman his tale. She might not be the girlfriend, but she probably knew every other madam in Trinidad. Hopefully she would spread the word to the right party, so that Buoy would come looking for him without Longarm having to go chase the man down.

Finally he collected his hat from the girl in the footman's livery and allowed himself to be escorted out into the night.

Chapter 31

"Custis! How wonderful to see you again, dear."

In his mind Longarm's first reaction was Oh, shit, what are you doing here? but all he said aloud was "Brenda. How have you been?"

"I'm doing well, thank you. I'm moving up in the world. Managing this house now for . . . well, for a certain business-minded gentleman who prefers to remain nameless."

They were standing in the foyer of one of Trinidad's whorehouses, this one not so fancy. Brenda—he hated to admit it, but he had forgotten her last name—was an acquaintance from Denver five . . . no, make it six years ago.

Longarm drew closer to the slender, fortyish madam and took her by the arm. He faked a smile, leaned down, and in a low voice said, "Nameless can be a good thing, Brenda. I'd appreciate it if you wouldn't bandy mine around none. Better yet, don't be saying anything about what I do for a living, will you?"

Brenda's brown eyes went wide. "Do you mean . . . Oh, my. You're here undercover?"

"Not exactly. Um, sort of, that is. I just . . . Look,

Brenda, don't say nothing about me, all right?"

"Yes, whatever you say, Custis." Her expression was serious when she reached up and lightly touched his cheek. "You are such a dear man. I would do anything for you. I hope you know that. Custis, could I ask a favor of *you*?"

"You know I'd do anything for you that I can, Brenda. Are you in trouble again?"

She blushed and glanced downward, then met his eyes once more. "No trouble. Not this time, dear."

There had been a time, back in Denver, when Brenda was in deep trouble. Her pimp had sold her to a buyer from some foreign country where she was destined to be placed very much against her will into a sultan's harem or some such—Longarm never had quite gotten all of it straight in his mind. She managed to pull free of the pair of swarthy buyers and threw herself at Longarm's feet, begging sanctuary. His badge and his six-gun had provided it.

Now that frightened, sobbing young woman was self-possessed and mature. And still lovely, albeit in a different, almost ladylike manner. He smiled at her.

"Custis, you won't mind doing me another favor? You really won't?"

"Another? I don't remember a first one."

"You know when I mean."

"Oh, that. That don't count. It was in the line o' duty. Sort of."

"It counts to me, Custis. It counts in my heart."

"Anyway, girl, you know if I can do something for you, I will. What is it that you're wanting?"

"Come back to my suite? Have dinner with me. You know how much I like people." He knew no such thing, but he did not disabuse her of the idea that he knew much about her, when in truth he did not. Better to keep his mouth shut. "But I'm in authority here. I can't be friends with the whores and control them too. It's the same with the house help. I have to stay apart from all of them, and it makes me so lonely there are times I think I should quit managing the girls and go back to being one of them."

Longarm bent down and lightly kissed Brenda's forehead. "Not that I think you should do such a thing, girl, but you're sure still pretty enough to draw top money."

She laughed. "Thank you, Custis. I was feeling terribly blue. Then you came in and I started feeling better immediately. Do say that you will stay. Please?"

"That's a mighty easy favor to grant. Of course I'll stay." He had already had his dinner at Mrs. Garza's boardinghouse, but he could handle another bite now. Besides, Brenda was in a position to help him if she proved willing. If she knew or knew of Billy Buoy herself, that was fine. If she did not, she might be able to pass the word to the other madams and get the information back to Longarm.

Could be there was a glimmer of hope for Neal Bird after all.

Longarm smiled and offered his arm to Brenda. "Just show me the way, darlin'. I'm with you."

Chapter 32

Brenda paused to give instructions to her cook, then led Longarm to the back of the house, where a tiny room barely larger than a walk-in closet served as both her office and her bedroom. Her suite, she had called it. Brenda, it seemed, had a sense of humor.

Small as the room was, it held a cluttered rolltop desk, a wardrobe, and a rumpled cot. And it did have a door that could be closed. And locked.

As soon as that door was shut, Brenda turned and came into Longarm's arms. She raised her mouth to his and kissed him with a hunger she never showed in the past.

She took him by the hand and pulled him toward the cot, shedding clothes as she went.

Longarm glanced back toward the door. "What about, um, won't somebody be comin' with that supper you said you wanted?"

Brenda giggled. "I told her to bring supper for two. But not for an hour or two. I'm not to be disturbed until then." She reached up and began unbuttoning his shirt. Longarm unbuckled his gunbelt and laid it on top of some papers on Brenda's desk.

"Sit down, dear, so I can pull your boots off."

He sat on the side of the cot and Brenda knelt before him. She tugged one stovepipe boot off and then the other, set them aside, and quickly unbuttoned his trousers.

"Raise up for a second," she instructed. He did so, and Brenda pulled his britches and his drawers down together.

"Oh, my," she said as she peered at his erection. "I had forgotten what a lovely prick you have, dear."

Longarm smiled. He touched Brenda's cheek, stroked her temple, and placed the tips of two fingers under her chin. Gently, he eased her forward. She rocked toward him. Cupped his balls in the palm of one hand, while with the other she fondled his cock.

"It really is so very pretty, isn't it?"

That did not seem the sort of question that needed an answer, so Longarm remained silent while Brenda contemplated his pecker. After a moment she leaned forward and pressed her cheek against his shaft. With a sigh she rose up a little higher. She ran the tip of her tongue over him.

"That feels . . . Damn, girl, that does feel good."

Brenda smiled.

She took the head of his cock very loosely into her mouth and swirled her tongue around and around over it, then down the shaft again. She pulled his foreskin back and again licked him. With her other hand she tickled the sensitive flat between his balls and his asshole.

Longarm touched the back of her head to ease her down onto him, and she complied, taking him into her mouth, engulfing him in the warmth of her mouth and then, pushing harder, on through into her throat. Longarm arched his back and closed his eyes and gave himself over to the sensations Brenda was giving him.

She closed her lips tight around him and began to suck. Hard. And then harder still.

"If you . . . Oh, shit . . . If you . . . ain't careful I'm gonna . . . gonna come right quick."

Brenda mumbled something, whatever she was trying to say muffled by the presence of his dick in her mouth.

"What?"

She pulled off him and tried again. "I want you to come in my mouth, dear. I want to taste it. I want to drink it. Then you'll last longer the second time." She grinned. "When I get you inside my pussy."

"Can't argue with that logic, can I?" he agreed.

Brenda bent her head over him again and began loudly sucking while she teased his balls with both hands.

With no reason to hold back, Longarm once more closed his eyes and let the sensations wash over and through him.

He felt the building pressure in his balls, the thrill of release, and the wild explosion of his juices flooding into Brenda's mouth as she continued to suck and pull at him.

This, he thought, was not an unpleasant way to conduct an interrogation.

"Come up here, babe. I want to hold you," he said.

"All right but give me a minute. I want to be naked. I want to feel your body against mine. And then, mister, I want to feel that cock inside me. You don't know how bad I want that now."

"Oh, I think we can manage that, ma'am. An' then we can have us a talk while you're havin' your dinner."

Brenda stood and quickly shed the rest of her clothes. She was still a beautiful woman, Longarm saw, clothed or otherwise. Her tits sagged a little now, whereas they had been firm and perky when he knew her before. Her butt was not as tight nor her belly quite as flat. But all in all she was lovely.

"Well?" she asked when he was done looking her over.

Longarm winked at her. "I like what I see, ma'am. I like it just fine."

"Show me how much you like it, Custis." She came to him then, her body lithe and active, her pussy wet and ready.

He was quite happy to show her.

Chapter 33

"Wait here, dear. Don't get dressed yet."

"Wha . . . ?"

"Trust me." The smile she gave him was positively feline. But pleased. Hell, she should be, he thought. He couldn't begin to count the number of times Brenda had come in the past . . . what had it been? Couple hours, maybe? Time well spent, whatever it was. "Trust me."

Brenda stood and took a housecoat down from a hook on the wall. She covered herself, then let herself out into the hallway. Longarm lay back on her narrow, sweat-soaked bed and closed his eyes. He might have nodded off for a few minutes, because the next thing he knew, Brenda was bumping and thumping at the door.

"Help me, Custis. Hold the door for me, please," she called through the closed door.

Oh, yes, he recalled. The original reason they came back here was to have a late supper. And she had said something to the cook on their way in. This must be the result of that instruction.

Even so, Longarm reached for his gunbelt and took hold of the worn, chipped grips of his Colt before he turned the latch and pulled the door open. Brenda, smiling, wheeled a cart into the already tiny room and pushed it into a niche beside the rolltop desk. He got the impression that this was a common enough procedure. Probably she kept herself aloof from the working girls even when it came to meals. A lonely life indeed for such a friendly person, he thought.

"What do you have there?" he asked, eyeing the polished metal domes that covered a number of dishes.

"You'll see, but first I want you to lie down."

"I can do that." He set his gunbelt aside and stretched out on the cot.

Brenda reached under the cart to a lower shelf and took the lid off a pottery jar. From it she extracted a wet washcloth. Kneeling between Longarm's legs, she proceeded to clean him with a succession of what proved to be hot—almost uncomfortably so—cloths. By the time she was done with that, his cock, which he had thought was used up to the point of being dead for days to come, was standing tall again.

"Custis dear, do you want me to take care of that for you?" she asked, fingering his shaft and running a fingernail lightly over the tip of his dick.

"Girl, you got work to do and so do I. We'd best wait on that." He grinned. "But I'd like to reserve the right to change my mind about that sometime soon."

Brenda laughed. "Any time, Custis. For you, dear, any time at all."

He got dressed while Brenda laid out a light supper, arranging the dishes on the cart and on the surface of her rolltop. Then the two of them sat on the edge of her bed with plates in hand to have their meal.

"Could I ask your help with something, Brenda?"

"Of course, dear. Anything. I hope you know that."

Longarm nodded, swallowed a bite of cheese, and said, "I'm here looking for a man named Billy Buoy. B-u-o-y. Or Billy Boy B-o-y, as he calls himself most often. D'you know him?"

She thought for a moment, then shook her head. "The name is not familiar. What does he look like?"

"I've never seen the man," Longarm told her. "He's said to be in his late twenties or thereabouts. Works cattle for a living. The fellas I talked to about him say he has dark hair and favors a short beard, but that was a couple years ago. He might could be clean shaved now. Hell, for all I know he could've gone bald by now."

"And you want to arrest him?"

Longarm shook his head. "No, I want to talk to him. He's a witness that might have information about a murder that took place a while back. All I want from him is the truth about what happened then. Oh, and I forgot to tell you why it's here that I'm looking for him. He claimed to have a girlfriend who's a madam in one of the whorehouses here in Trinidad."

"A madam, you say?"

"That's what I was told. I can't swear that it's the truth, but it was told to someone for true."

"I can ask around for you, Custis. I know most of the other ladies in this business. I will certainly find out for you if I can. Billy Boy, you said."

"Uh-huh."

"Pass me that bacon would you, please?"

It occurred to Longarm that he had long since missed the ten o'clock deadline Mrs. Garza imposed for her guests to come in. By now he would be locked out of his room.

He chuckled. And explained the problem. "So I was thinking," he concluded, "that maybe I could bunk in here and then in the morning, when you and your girls shut down, maybe you could come and us have a little morning delight before I go off about my work and you get you some sleep."

"Morning delight, is it?"

"Sure would be a delight, ma'am." He reached out and cupped his hand over her breast. He gently squeezed.

"Morning delight sounds just fine," Brenda said. "Now be quiet and finish your supper so I can get back out there and see that my whores don't get themselves in trouble somehow. I swear, cowboys have it so easy herding cattle. If they want a challenge, let them try to ride herd on a bunch of lazy whores for a living."

"I bet you do a right good job of it though," he told her. Not that he had any idea what a whorehouse madam was required to do or how well Brenda might do it, but it was the sort of thing he thought she would like to hear.

The comment did seem to perk her up. She smiled and sat up a little straighter while they finished eating.

Chapter 34

"Could I trouble you for a pot of hot water, Mrs. Garza?" Longarm asked in his most polite and inoffensive voice.

The lady sniffed. Loudly. "I daresay I should refuse you. Why, you should be ashamed of yourself, staying out all night like that."

Longarm kept his eyes down, examining the old biddy's shoes instead of meeting her glare. "I was out visiting with friends last night when I saw it was past ten. I knew you'd be abed by then, and I sure didn't want to come bother you to open the door for me, so I just stayed out. Figured that was the best thing to do under the circumstances."

Mrs. Garza sniffed again. But more softly this time. "If it happens again, young man, you might keep in mind that I complain about the way you boys stay out late, but I will always open the door for you."

"Why, thank you, ma'am. I didn't know, but I sure appreciate it."

"Have you had your breakfast?"

"Yes, ma'am."

"Then you might like some coffee. It's over there on the stove."

"Just the hot water if that wouldn't be too much of a bother."

She sniffed. But she was almost smiling now. "No bother at all. There are some kettles in that closet. Help yourself to one and draw your water from the reservoir. It should be nice and hot. Is there anything else you need? Soap? Towels? Anything at all?"

"No, ma'am. I think I have all that in my room already. Except for the water. The kettles are in that closet, you say? Thank you, ma'am. I surely do appreciate you."

By then she was really smiling.

Longarm carried his kettle of hot water back to his room and poured some into the basin that was already there. He thought about shaving himself, then realized that would be a mistake and used the water to bathe himself instead. After his morning delight with Brenda he was getting more than a little gamey. Plenty sticky too.

Not that he was complaining.

He washed, dressed again, and strapped his gunbelt in place. He was feeling on top of the world except for still needing to find Billy Buoy. And Brenda would very likely be able to help there.

Longarm returned the kettle to Mrs. Garza's kitchen, thanking the landlady when he did so, then walked out into the town. He spotted a barber's pole on the street, on the cattlemen's side of town, and headed toward it.

There were already half a dozen gents sitting on chairs ranged along the wall, men waiting for their morning shaves, and two barbers working to satisfy that demand. Longarm picked up a rumpled newspaper from a rack beside the door and chose one of the few empty seats.

The newspaper was one he had already read on the train coming down to Trinidad, but at the moment he was not interested in the news on the printed page anyway, but in surreptitiously listening in on the conversations around him. Not that he expected Buoy's name to be mentioned, but he had long since noticed that sometimes you can learn more by opening your ears than by opening your mouth.

More than an hour later—and better informed than he ever wanted to be about the state of available graze along the Purgatory River east of Trinidad—it became Longarm's turn in one of the barber chairs.

"Good morning, sir." The barber, a thin man wearing spectacles, shook out his striped sheet and pulled it up beneath Longarm's chin. "Shave and a haircut, sir?"

"Just the shave, please."

"Would you like me to trim that mustache for you too?"

"You might thin it down a little but keep it full. If you know what I mean."

The barber smiled. "Oh, I believe I do, yes." Longarm never ceased to be amazed how much attention a good mustache required. Near about as much time as a woman put in on her hair, he sometimes thought. That was an exaggeration, perhaps. But not much of one.

The barber picked up his scissors and a slender comb and worked on Longarm's mustache first, snipping and fluffing and snipping some more. Then he picked up his soap mug and shaving brush and got down to the main business at hand.

"You wouldn't happen to know a man name of Billy Boy, would you?" Longarm asked. "I'm in town hopin' to give him a message."

The barber scowled in thought, then shook his head. "I'm not familiar with the gentleman."

"How 'bout these fellas? You think some one of them might know the man?" Longarm suggested.

The barber shrugged, then raised his voice and addressed the four men who had come in after Longarm and were still waiting for their turns in the chairs. "Anybody here know a fellow called Billy Boy?"

There was no response from the other customers, so after a moment the barber said, "Sorry, mister. I'm afraid I can't help you."

"Thanks all right, friend. I appreciate you trying," Longarm told him.

The fellow finished Longarm's shave and swept the sheet away from him with a flourish. Longarm stood and gave the man a quarter for the fifteen-cent job, waving his change away. He retrieved his hat from the rack beside the front door and stepped out onto the sidewalk again.

"Hey. Mister." The voice was low. It came from the mouth of the narrow alley that ran between the barbershop and a millinery next door.

Chapter 35

Before he stepped around the corner into that alley, Longarm palmed his Colt. He held it low by his side where it would not be easily noticed.

"What is it?" he asked as he moved into the mouth of the alley.

Two men stood there, cowhands by the look of them but rather dandy, as both wore tooled leather cuffs, fancy stitched boots, and hats that did not have sweat stains around the crown. Both were armed, but their revolvers were holstered.

"Something you boys want?"

The nearer of the two, a lean fellow with a scab at the corner of his mouth, nodded. "We got a message for you."

"All right. Deliver it." Longarm's thumb was draped over the hammer of his .45. Not that he was expecting trouble, but a fellow never knows.

"We heard tell you're looking for a friend of ours, fella name of Billy Boy."

It was Longarm's turn to nod. "Ayuh. You say he's a friend o' yours. Good friend?"

"Good enough."

"Then you should ought to take me to him."

"How well do you know him, mister?"

"Me," Longarm shrugged, "I don't know him at all. Never laid eyes on the man."

"Then how is it you're looking for him?"

"I have a message for the man."

"You can tell it to me and I'll pass it on."

There was nothing threatening in either man's posture or outward expression, so Longarm slipped his Colt back into the leather and said, "The message is for him. I'll not be telling it to anybody else. Will you take me to him or at the least tell him about me being here?"

The skinny cowhand turned and looked at his companion, who grunted softly, hesitated for a moment, and then nodded. "We can take you to him," the second man said. "Billy is about an hour's ride from here."

"Then I'd better go rent me a horse," Longarm said. "I come down on the train."

"All right. Meet us at the east end of town, close by the river. We'll take you out there."

The other one put in, "Half an hour from now."

"Fair enough," Longarm said. He touched the brim of his hat and turned away. If he was going to be traveling out of town, he wanted to have his gear with him, what little of it he had brought along.

He hurried back to Mrs. Garza's rooming house and let himself in. He collected his vest and coat and put them on, and took the carpetbag too, as a person in his position could rarely be certain about being able to return to a place once he left it. He only wished he had his own saddle and rifle as well.

There were two livery stables in Trinidad, at least there were two that he had noticed. There could be more, but if so, he did not know where. The establishment close to the railroad seemed to go heavy on wagons and buggies and the like, while the stable at the east end of town had more in the way of saddle stock. Longarm headed east from Mrs. Garza's house.

The hostler at the livery looked Longarm over, assessing his city clothing and the military boots with heels meant for walking. "You'll be wanting something gentle, I expect."

Longarm grinned. "It's good of you to watch out for my welfare, friend, but what I'm needing is more in the way of staying power than gentle. I don't care if the sonuvabitch has fire coming out of its nostrils, just so he don't wear down like so many livery horses do."

"You're sure you can handle a good horse? Can you look me in the eye and tell me you never been throwed off?"

"Have I ever been throwed? Hell yes I have. So have you. Only way not to is to not ride but take a buggy." The grin flashed again. "Come to think of it, I've seen some idjits throwed out of buggies too. But I hope I ain't like that."

"I got a good horse back here, mister, but he ain't been rode in the better part of a week. He might be a little rank to start with, but he can go all day and half the night too."

"Let's put a saddle on him then," Longarm said.

The horse the hostler led him to was a short-coupled, muscular gray with wide-set eyes and a bull neck. Longarm liked the fact that it accepted bit and saddle without difficulty and that it showed more curiosity than fear.

"You want to take him to one of the pens out back and work him on a longe line to wear some of the tomfoolery out of him first?" the hostler offered.

"No need for that," Longarm said. No time for it either, he thought silently to himself. Those two cowboys were waiting down by the river. And every minute that passed put Neal Bird that much closer to hanging.

He adjusted the stirrup leathers long enough for his legs, wadded his carpetbag down as small as he could get it, and lashed it in place behind the cantle of the battered old livery stable saddle, then led the gray out into the street.

The gray was honest enough. It allowed Longarm time to find his seat and get his boots into the stirrups before it let the rank out.

The horse snorted loudly, blowing snot and maybe some flames too. Or so it felt from Longarm's perspective. The gray dropped its head, braced its legs wide apart, and then exploded so hard it felt like it was coming apart, with bits of hair and hide flying in all directions.

Longarm concentrated on clinging on with legs and arms alike. He clamped down so hard with his legs that he worried he might break the gray's ribs, and he was not too proud to hang onto the saddle horn as well. If he could have reached the horse's neck with his teeth, he would have held on there too.

Man and beast started off down the road like that, the gray touching earth only now and then and Longarm being flung every which way but off.

Helluva ride, Longarm thought. Just one helluva ride.

Chapter 36

Longarm stepped off the gray, leaned down, and tore a large handful of grass out of the ground. He wrapped the grass stems around his hand and used that makeshift brush to rub the gray down a little lest the powerful animal come down sick from drying off too slowly.

The two cowboys rode up and stopped close by. The lean fellow, whom Longarm dubbed Skinny in his mind since no names had been offered, asked, "Man, how'd you get him so sweaty in just a half mile or so?"

Longarm looked up from working on the horse and grinned. "Oh, some bird came along an' insulted him, so he went to tryin' to catch the damn thing. I don't know what it was all about, though. Probably something to do with females. That's usually the problem when any sort of animal gets itself into a jam."

"You can say that again. You ready to go, mister?"

"Sure 'nuff." Longarm tossed his now soggy wad of grass aside, turned the stirrup to his liking, and stepped astride the gray. "Ready if you are."

"Stick with us then," said the other one, whom Longarm had begun thinking of as Fats. "This won't take too long."

Skinny and Fats booted their horses, both of which carried the V Bar brand, and set off at an easy lope down along the flow of the Purgatory, generally known as the Picketwire. The north bank of the river was lined with scattered small farms and failing homesteads. After half an hour or so the two cowboys angled north, away from the river, with Longarm following in their dust.

Once they got out onto the grass, away from the homesteads, Fats drew rein. Skinny followed suit and Longarm stopped beside them.

"I got to take a piss," Fats declared. "Let's all get down and take a breather." Without waiting for anyone else to object, Fats dismounted. He unbuttoned his britches, pulled his dick out, and began to drain the snake.

Longarm did not feel any need to piss, but he did take the opportunity to get down and light a cheroot. He checked the gray's cinch and patted the horse on the neck. The animal had not given him a moment's trouble once it had worked the kinks out of its spine back there in town.

"We're ready if you are, mister."

Longarm nodded, gathered his reins over the gray's neck, and stepped into the saddle.

His two guides led the way at an easy pace for the next forty-five minutes or so, until they came to what looked like some outfit's line camp. It was not much, just a dugout with a low roof and a small pen where a burro and a small mare stood. What looked like a natural seep had been boxed and a hand pump installed to provide water.

"You can get down here, mister. This is the place."

All three men dismounted. Skinny gathered up all the reins and led the three horses to the pen, while Fats motioned Longarm toward the dugout. "In there," Fats said.

Longarm grunted and headed for the dugout. He had to bend down to get through the doorway.

Just as he did so, he felt a terrible blow on the back of his head. A lightning bolt of pain and white light shot through his skull. But only for an instant.

And then everything went black.

Longarm was out cold before he had time to feel himself falling.

Chapter 37

Longarm woke to discover that the lightning bolt had come to stay. His head felt like it had been split in two. And the two halves rubbed in salt. The pain in the back of his head pulsed and throbbed with each and every heartbeat, while a lesser pain stung his chin and the right side of his face.

So some son of a bitch—it had to be the man he'd dubbed Fats—had whacked him from behind. He remembered that much. Then, although he did not actually remember it, he must have fallen forward. Onto his face, more than likely. That would account for the chin and right side of his face.

But where . . . He tried to move and could not. His hands seemed to have been tied behind him with something hard and . . . now that he thought of it—now that he *could* think again—he seemed to be immobilized with handcuffs. His own handcuffs, he guessed. The bastards probably thought that was funny. Turn the tables on the stupid marshal and do it with his own damn handcuffs. Sure. Longarm would think it was funny too if it was somebody else's handcuffs. As things stood now, though . . .

He groaned and tried, without much success, to sit up.

"All right," he mumbled. "Who are you and what do you want?" He lifted his head as best he could and blinked a few times to clear his eyes, then looked around.

He was inside the dugout. Fats and his pal Skinny were sitting at a small table. From his position on the dirt floor Longarm could not see the top of the table, but Skinny picked up first a playing card and then a coffee cup. He reached over and placed the card, then picked up another. Playing some form of solitaire, Longarm guessed.

"Did you say something?" Fats asked, standing and moving over to stop by Longarm's side.

"Yeah," Longarm said, his voice stronger now that he seemed to be getting a handle on this waking up thing. "I asked what this is all about. Maybe you're thinking I got a lot of money. If that's your game, then you are gonna be awful disappointed."

Fats squatted down beside him and peered into Longarm's face for a moment. "You don't understand at all, do you?"

"No. I said that already. But I don't have much money. I'm just here to deliver a message to a fella, that's all."

"You're a liar," Fats said. "You know how I know that for a fucking fact? I'll tell you how. I seen you before. You didn't see me, I'm sure, but I seen you one afternoon in the courthouse lobby outside Neal Bird's trial for murdering that old son of a bitch Tipton. You were pointed out to me then as the deputy United States marshal that brought Neal in. I don't remember your name, mister, but I know for sure that you're a deputy marshal and that you been lying to me about this message shit. You came down here to arrest me, not to deliver no message."

"Arrest you? Why the hell would I do that?" Longarm protested.

"You don't know? You aren't shitting me and really don't know?"

"Mister, right now I got no idea what in hell you are talking about."

"I am talking about you knowing who I am," Fats said.

"I don't have a fucking clue," Longarm told him.

Fats chuckled. He stood and turned to his partner. "Mike, would you perform the introductions here?"

Skinny, whose name seemed to be Mike, quit his card game for a moment and turned in his chair, bending forward and planting his elbows on his knees so he could look Longarm in the face. He laughed and said, "Mister, my good friend here is William Buoy. But us friends of his usually call him Billy Boy."

"Well, shit," Longarm grumbled.

"Ain't that the truth," Buoy said.

"So who are you, mister?" Mike asked.

There did not seem much point in remaining silent on that subject, Longarm thought, so he told them.

"And what is it brings you down here?" Buoy asked.

"Help me sit up, would you? It ain't so comfortable down here."

"That wasn't the question, but all right." Buoy took hold of Longarm's shoulder and tugged. He pulled Longarm upright so he could sit with his back against a wall faced with rock. The stone was cold, but leaning against it felt much better than lying in the dirt had.

"Thanks."

"Now, tell me, Long. Why are you after me? I haven't knocked over any post offices or mail pouches or anything like that."

"I'm here because a friend of yours is fixing to hang unless I find cause to reverse that judgment. I'm here to ask can you help save Neal Bird from a hangman's noose."

Buoy stepped back and resumed his seat at the card table. He shook his head and said, "Now, that is just the damnedest thing I ever did hear. A fucking law dog coming all this way to try and save the life of a low-down murderer. Who, by the way, is no particular friend of mine."

"You could have told me all this in town," Longarm said, "and saved us both a lot of trouble."

"Yeah, well, maybe I thought you was coming after me for . . . uh, for something or other. Point is, now it's too late to back up and start over." He laughed again. "Now that we got you, Long, we're kind of stuck with you."

"Dammit, Billy, shoot the son of a bitch and get it over with."

"Don't be in such a hurry, Mike. We got him. He ain't going anywhere or doing anything. Not until we say so. I'm wondering if maybe there's some way for us to bene- fit from having him. You know, like, oh, a finder's fee or a reward or some such of a thing."

"Don't try to get cute with this guy, Billy. Just shoot him and be done with it."

"No. I don't think so. Let me think about this. We can always put a bullet in his head, but first give me time to think about it."

Longarm considered his options. And decided to keep his mouth shut. Inside, though, he was rooting for Billy Boy's approach instead of Mike's.

Chapter 38

"Look, Billy, I just don't feel comfortable talking about this with him listening. How about we take a walk outside. We can check on the horses and talk without him listening in."

Billy Boy shrugged. "It's okay with me, but pick up his pistol and stick it in your belt, will you? I know those handcuffs are secure, but I wouldn't feel comfortable leaving a gun around."

Mike stood and stretched and picked up Longarm's familiar Colt from the table where it had been lying out of sight. He stuck the revolver into his waistband and reached for his hat.

"Can I ask you one thing before you go out?" Longarm said.

Buoy paused and asked, "What about?"

"It's about that thing up at Tipton's store, the deal Bird is about to swing for. No bullshit now, what really happened up there?"

"Are you real sure you want me to answer that, Deputy? You know, if the answer turned out to be something that would be bad for me . . . and I tell you about it now . . . then Mike and me would pretty much have to put that bullet in your brain. It'd be better from your point of view to not know. That way there'd at least be some chance of us deciding to turn you loose here an' not risk a murder charge 'cause right now the only thing anybody could bring against us is robbery. And as a federal deputy you don't know nor care shit about that. Isn't that right?"

"Ayuh. It is," Longarm agreed.

"So, y'see there, it's in your own best interests for me to ignore that question of yours."

"Yeah. You're right," Longarm said.

"C'mon, Mike. Let's go have us that talk." Buoy led the way out through the low doorway and let the cowhide that covered it drop closed over the entrance, blacking out nearly all the inside, as there were no windows and the only lamp in the room had not been lit.

Longarm was left alone in the dark, sitting on the dirt floor with his hands cuffed behind him.

He did not for a moment consider that the two men might return only to set him free again. When they came back, they would surely intend to kill him, and his job right now was to keep that from happening.

Somehow.

And he better come up with that plan damned quick, because it wouldn't take any longer than the time it takes for a man to smoke a quirley and the two would be back. Likely with guns in hand.

Chapter 39

First things first, he thought. And that was to get out of these damned handcuffs.

Longarm struggled up from his sitting position and, with difficulty, wound up on his knees. He reached down and back, straining to get the chain of the handcuffs past his boots. If he could do that he could get his hands in front of his body. From there it would be an easy, down-hill slide to get his hands free. *If* he could get his . . . damned . . . hands in front.

Much easier said than done, though. No amount of pushing and straining seemed enough. He just could not do it.

What he needed to do was to shorten his legs so he could work the cuffs past his feet.

And, come to think of it, there was a way to do that.

Longarm flopped over onto his back again and hastily kicked off his boots. That removed an inch or so that the chain had to travel in order to pass underneath his feet.

In his stocking feet then, Longarm once again wriggled up onto his knees. This time he managed to drag the chain past his heels. The steel manacles pressing into his hands hurt like hell, but all he could do was to grit his teeth and keep pressing.

He rolled over onto his back, doubled his legs up until he thought they might break, and pulled.

The chain linking the separate manacles rolled reluctantly over the ball of his right foot.

And off.

He felt like shouting. Except he was not out of the woods yet. Mike and Billy Boy were outside somewhere, and Longarm was far from being ready for their return. He yanked again and pulled the chain over his left foot also. The handcuffs were now, thank goodness, in front of his body instead of behind. It made all the difference.

He jumped to his feet, stumbled once, and grabbed the edge of the table to right himself, then dipped two fingers into the watch pocket that had been sewn into the waist of his corduroys. Longarm was smiling when he extracted a handcuff key.

From there it was a matter of seconds to release first the left cuff and then, even more easily, the right.

He returned the key to its tiny pocket and the handcuffs to his coat pocket.

His Colt was gone, but his derringer . . . He patted his vest . . . It was gone too, dammit. One of them must have robbed him of his watch and chain, with the little pistol attached, while he was unconscious.

He looked quickly around the dugout for a weapon, any sort of weapon. There was nothing at hand intended for such use, but . . .

Longarm tipped the card table onto its side, ignoring the oil lamp that slid off and shattered on the floor and the sheaf of cardboard playing cards that were scattered onto the dirt.

He took hold of the nearest table leg and pushed down sharply, giving the leg his full weight. It snapped off, and Longarm smiled. Perfect. What he had in hand now was a club, about thirty inches in length and with reasonably sharp edges where the four flat-planed sides met.

He retrieved his boots and pulled them on—when it comes to any sort of physical confrontation a man in his bare feet is always at a disadvantage—then hefted his makeshift club and crouched beside the low doorway.

Billy Boy or Mike, at least one of them, would be back soon enough with the intention to shoot him dead. That was the decision they would inevitably come to in their palaver out there. It pretty much had to be. Either they came back and gave themselves up to Longarm for him to arrest them or they returned and put a bullet in his brain. Those were really the only choices open to them. And Longarm was under no illusions about which of the two they would pick.

He laughed, feeling full of himself now even though on the face of it he ought to have considered his position more than a little precarious, one man armed only with a chunk of wood facing two men armed with at least one Colt revolver.

The thing was, though, he was still alive. More than that, he was alive and free. By Longarm's reckoning, that put him ahead of the game, and those sons of bitches out there would be well advised to step back inside and give themselves up, not so much to Custis Long as to The Law.

Longarm took a renewed grip on his club and waited.

Chapter 40

Good. He heard the crunch of gravel being ground under-
foot as at least one of them headed for the doorway into
the dugout. Longarm listened closely. One, he thought,
followed by the other.

They would be coming in fat and sassy, thinking they
were in the catbird seat. All they had to do was to step
inside, take aim, and blow Longarm's brains out with one
well-placed .45 slug. Easiest thing in the world.

Except Custis Long was not lying on the floor, safely
trussed up with his own damned handcuffs. He was a free
man now, damn them, and he had no plan to make anything easy for them. Far from it!

The footsteps reached the narrow depression that led
down to the dugout. They slowed, then stopped for a moment. Longarm was not sure but thought he heard some
whispering, then the one set of footsteps moved closer.

Longarm took a fresh grip on his club and leaned close
to the front wall of the dugout.

The cowhide that served as a door was swept aside and
a man's head and shoulders pushed inside.

It was almost too easy, Longarm thought. The son of a

bitch was bent low to get through the small opening. That presented the back of his neck just as pretty as you please.

Longarm raised the table leg and struck with all the force and speed he possessed.

There was a loud crack—the table leg breaking? he didn't know for sure—and the man he'd hit dropped face-down like a poleaxed shoat ready for bleeding and butchering.

Mike, Longarm saw. It was the sidekick Mike who lay there motionless in the middle of the entrance.

Longarm took no time to admire his handiwork. Quickly he knelt and retrieved the Remington six-gun Mike'd had ready in his hand. The Remington was already cocked. Ready indeed, Longarm thought. He had been a hairsbreadth away from being murdered himself.

He pushed the beef hide aside, leveled the .45, and shot Billy Buoy, who had been following close behind his pal Mike.

Buoy screamed, tried to back away, and fell writhing to the ground. "You gut-shot me, you son of a bitch. You didn't give me no chance at all, you just up and gut-shot me."

Buoy seemed much more interested in his own pain than in Longarm or in Mike, so Longarm took a moment to kneel and check Mike to see if he had a pulse. He did not. The man was cooling meat. The whack Longarm gave him must have popped his skull off his spine, and he'd gone out like a candle flame in a sudden gust of wind. Likely never knew a thing, Longarm thought.

Mike's partner, on the other hand, was damn sure aware of having been shot. Buoy was lying out there on his back wailing and crying and carrying on something awful.

"Hey. You! Pay attention, asshole. Throw that shooter away. Toss it out to the side, to where you can't reach it, or I'll start at your stinking feet and work my way up till I shoot you plumb to pieces. You don't think I'll do it, just try me."

"You bastard," Buoy shouted back. "You've gut-shot me, I say."

"Yes, I guess I have. And I'll shoot you a helluva lot more if you don't do what I say. Now, pitch that pistol away."

Buoy calmed down and shut up enough to do as Longarm said. He threw his Colt off to the side.

"Now the other one," Longarm prodded.

"I don't have . . ."

"Yes, you do, asshole. You have my Colt shoved in your waistband. I saw it there when I shot you. Took care to not ruin my gun when I put that slug into you." That part was a bit of a fabrication. No pistol, or any other mere possession, was important enough that Longarm would even think about preserving it when his own life was at stake. "Toss it too." When Buoy did not instantly comply, Longarm added, "Right damn now or I start shooting again."

Buoy dragged the Colt out of his waistband and rather weakly pitched it aside.

"Where's my derringer?" Longarm demanded. These were not people to take chances with.

"Mike had the little gun. Your watch too. He liked the way they was strung together."

"Okay. Lay there an' bleed while I check your partner."

Longarm bent down again and rolled Mike onto his side. Just as Buoy had said, Longarm's watch and derringer were in his pocket. So was Longarm's wallet, along with his

folding money. He guessed Billy Buoy had taken possession of his hard money. Fuckers hadn't even had the decency to kill him before they robbed him. He retrieved his
things from Mike, then had to step on the corpse in order to
get through the doorway and outside to where Buoy was
once again bawling about how bad he hurt.

Longarm picked up the assorted firearms that were lying about, brushed the dirt and grit off his own Colt, and
shoved it back into its leather. Mike's Remington and
Buoy's Colt he pitched into the water sump. Then he
walked back and knelt beside Buoy.

He pulled the man's shirt open, then loosened his belt
and the buttons on his denim jeans and pushed them away
too. Longarm grunted. "Yep," he growled. "You're gut-
shot, all right. Can't nothing be done for a wound like
that. You're done for, Billy. Might as well count yourself a
dead man already. Oh, you'll lay here an' suffer. Suffer
something terrible. I seen it many and many a time. By
the end you'll be beggin' me to put my bullet in your
brain . . . you know, like you was gonna do to me . . . but
being a Christian sort, that's something I won't be able to
do. I'll set here and listen to you scream, but it'll be
against everything I believe in to put you out of your misery. That's a funny thing when you think about it. If you
was a gut-shot dog, nobody'd think a thing about me put-
ting you down. But you being a human critter, I just can't
do any such of a thing. You'll just have to lay here for the
next day, maybe as long as four or five days you'll lay
here, and suffer and scream and die from that bullet in
your guts."

"Then let me have a pistol. One bullet in it so you
know I won't shoot you. Let me kill myself. Have the
decency to do that, man. I'm begging you."

"Maybe . . . just maybe we could work something out," Longarm said.

"Anything. Please. Anything."

"Either of you boys have pen and ink in your saddle-bags?" Longarm asked.

Buoy's brow furrowed in puzzlement. "Pen and ink? What the hell would we carry something like that for?"

"I dunno," Longarm said. "I was just asking." He sighed. "I got me a pencil and some expense sheets in my carpetbag. I reckon we could use the back side of one of those for what I have in mind."

"I don't know what you're talking about," Buoy said.

"I'm talking about relieving you from the burden of dying so slow and painful like you are."

"You mean you'd do it? You'd give me my pistol with one bullet in it?"

"I might do that, Billy. But first I want to ask you some questions. Mind, though, I'm wanting truthful answers from you. The straight shit now or I'll let you lay here and die and hurt and scream until kingdom come."

"Anything," Buoy swore. "I'll tell you anything you want to know."

"Wait here," Longarm said, "whilst I go get that paper and pencil outta my carpetbag. Then we'll have us a real good talk."

Chapter 41

"I think this here dyin' declaration will do," Longarm said. "Those are admissible in court, y'know. Man thinks he's taking his last breaths, he's gonna tell the truth. Yes, sir, I can take this document with your signature at the bottom, I can take it to a judge up in Pueblo or Cañon City or thereabouts and have Neal Bird's conviction overturned. Guaranteed." Longarm stood, went to his rented horse, and tucked William Buoy's signed confession safely away.

Buoy, it seemed, was the one who'd murdered both the Indian woman and Jason Tipton, while Bird and Zenas Perch lay passed out inside Tipton's store. He did it, he claimed, because the Indian woman refused to suck his dick after he took it out of her ass. He killed her first, and when Tipton threatened to turn him in, he killed the store-keeper too.

"That wasn't fair," Buoy complained now. "She was just a lousy Injun. Wasn't like she was worth getting all worked up over."

"Do you want to add that to your confession?" Longarm asked. "About Tipton not being fair with you after you killed his woman, I mean."

"No, we've already used up all that paper," Buoy said. "If they want them to know, you can tell 'em." He snorted. "It ain't like there's anybody left to dispute what I say there."

"Except Neal Bird," Longarm said, "and he sure ain't gonna complain about you taking the hangman's noose off his neck."

"You'll tell him that I'm sorry, Long? You'll tell Neal that I done him wrong and I wanta apologize for that. It's just . . . you know. Better he should swing than me."

"Tell him yourself, Billy."

"Now, ain't that a shitty sort of joke. You know good and well that I'm laying here dying. I won't live long enough to tell him a damn thing. Nor anybody else for that matter."

"Uh-huh. So tell me, Bill, how are you feeling now?"

"Some better. I hurt like hell, but the bleeding has stopped. I guess it will be a while before the really bad pain hits me." He squeezed his eyes tight shut and shuddered. "They say once the pain starts, it is the awfulest pain there ever was. I don't want that. Now, do right by me, Long. Hand me my pistol so's I can keep myself from having to go through that. You promised, remember. And I've gave you what you wanted. You got my confession that takes Neal off the hook. He won't have to hang after all."

"Yeah, well . . . now that you've confessed to me, Billy, there's something I got to confess to you."

"What would that be, Marshal?"

"First off, I'm not gonna hand you any pistol, loaded or otherwise."

"Hey!" Buoy shouted. "You *promised*."

"Uh-huh. The thing is, Billy . . . I lied. I lied about let-ting you shoot yourself. Though maybe I should, as it'd save an awful lot of trouble. Still, it wouldn't be right. It'd go against my oath as a lawman. And the other thing . . . actually that's your fault as you're the one came up with the idea. I just went along with it."

"What the hell are you talking about, Long?" Buoy raised himself up a few inches on one elbow, winced at the pain that caused, and sank down onto his back again.

"What I'm saying, Billy, is that you ain't gut-shot. My bullet went into your side more than your belly. Likely busted your hip is why it hurts so blasted much. But you ain't gut-shot. I've seen more than my fair share of gut wounds. Them you can smell just about as much as you can see. They stink of shit that hasn't been passed out of the body yet. Stink something awful. Mostly don't bleed near as much as that wound of yours neither. No, Billy, I got to tell you, you're gonna live long enough to take Bird's place on that gallows up in Cañon City. I can pretty much promise you that." Longarm stood, his knee joints crackling. "Now, if you'll excuse me, Billy, I got to drape Mike over his saddle and take some fence rails to build you a travois so's I can get you back to Trinidad. I don't think you're quite up to riding astride right now."

"Long, you . . . you son of a bitch."

"Yeah, ain't that the shits, Billy? Ain't it just."

Longarm strode away, leaving Billy Buoy sputtering and cussing in the dirt behind him. Longarm was in a hurry now, a hurry to get back to town so he could get a wire off to the warden at the prison to make sure there wouldn't be a hanging, and another to Billy Vail to tell him the right murderer was in custody now and . . . There was just an awful lot to do and no time to waste doing it.

Watch for

LONGARM AND THE HOWLING MANIAC

the 377th novel in the exciting LONGARM
series from Jove

Coming in April!

LONGARM

GIANT-SIZED ADVENTURE FROM
AVENGING ANGEL LONGARM.

BY TABOR EVANS

penguin.com/actionwesterns

GIANT ACTION! GIANT ADVENTURE!

THE Gunsmith

J.R. ROBERTS

Little Sureshot And
The Wild West Show
(Gunsmith Giant #9)

Dead Weight
(Gunsmith Giant #10)

Red Mountain
(Gunsmith Giant #11)

The Knights of Misery
(Gunsmith Giant #12)

The Marshal from Paris
(Gunsmith Giant #13)

Lincoln's Revenge
(Gunsmith Giant #14)